1288

THE TALKING ROOM
ON MARIANNE HAUSER'S WORK:

On *Dark Dominion*:
"I cannot believe that the year will produce a richer, more original novel by any writer, new or old."

—Paul Engle in
Chicago Sunday Tribune

"Her novel shows her keen, original eye, her avid sense of life. It is an artistic novel, beautifully written, controlled by moral purpose. . ."

—Marguerite Young in *Vogue*

On *The Choir Invisible*.

"She lets the reader see (her characters) through her talented and ironic European eye, and writes the story with the wit and poetic horseplay of her adopted America."

—Mari Sandoz

"Author Hauser has a sharp eye and sure words for the homeliest of scenes."

—*Time*

On *Prince Ishmael*:

". . . a remarkably beautiful novel, rich in imagination, profound in insight, flawless in style."

—Richard Sullivan, *Chicago Tribune*

"She succeeds in fusing the fantastic and the ordinary. If her theme is informed with wit, her purpose is serious."

—Gene Baro, *New York Times*

(continued on back flap)

(continued from front flap)

"A strange, lyrical and haunting book, written with great vividness and beauty."

—Mary Renault

On *A Lesson in Music*:

"When people will tire of noise, crassness and vulgarity, they will hear the truly contemporary complexities of Marianne Hauser's superimpositions. A new generation, trained to imagery by the film, may appreciate her offbeat characters and skill in portraying the uncommon."

—Anaïs Nin, *The Novel of the Future*

other books by Marianne Hauser include

SHADOW PLAY IN INDIA, a novel
DARK DOMINION, a novel
THE CHOIR INVISIBLE, a novel
PRINCE ISHMAEL, a novel
A LESSON IN MUSIC, a collection of short stories

marianne hauser

THE TALKING ROOM

a novel

FICTION COLLECTIVE  NEW YORK

This publication is in part made possible with support from the
New York State Council on the Arts, Brooklyn College, and
Teachers & Writers Collaborative.

First Edition

Copyright © 1976 by Marianne Hauser
All rights reserved
Typesetting by New Hampshire Composition
Cover, jacket design by Joel Fisher and Adalberto Ortiz
Library of Congress Catalog No. 75-21557
ISBN:—0-914590-21-9—(paperbook)
ISBN:—0-914590-20-0—(hardcover)

Published by FICTION COLLECTIVE
distributed by George Braziller, Inc.
One Park Avenue
New York, N.Y. 10016

1903632

For W.K.

"in the black of us
there's a corridor
to the moon
hop, scotch & jump
one, two"

lee vassel

THE TALKING ROOM

Again I can hear their voices coming nonstop from the talking room downstairs. I hear them through the rumble of the trucks in the night rain as I lie on my back between moist sheets, listening. And I know they are talking about me. But they call me an idea.

B? She was your idea and don't you deny it.

Hush, dearest!

Your idea, not mine, the whole sick deal.

Hush! Hush!

Go hush yourself, you had it figured out to a T, planned parenthood—my aunt!—with me for mom and the test tube for pop, you really lapped that up, so sanitary, safer, you said, than some fly-by-night barfly, though anything will do. You said a little bastard is better than nothing, but make it snappy. Sweet Christ. You couldn't wait another second to play house.

You are drunk.

Just mellow, honey V, your mellow fellow. Sweet jesus why couldn't you play in your own sand box? Why did you have to stick your finger into my mud pie?

You're getting ugly, J.

Yes, I the J and you the V. We are initials. Our names got lost in the rumpled sheets, and what, my love, my dove, will they write on our communal headstone? Two capital letters? One capital lie? Here lies the lie, the fly, initial parents of one baby B, excuse the fart. The part you forced on me—I wasn't cut out for it, don't you see? I never learned to play mother. No football coach showed me.

There . . .Sit by me . . .Please, don't have another, lie down . . .Stretch out . . .I'll rub your back . . .There. There now . . .

Rub. Moan. But it's the wind I hear. The boats moan on

the river. They cry for the ocean. The voices in the talking room go dead. I've smothered them with my pillow, and maybe I invented them in any case. How would I know? It happened a long time ago, like yesterday. Those voices, I can turn them up or down like the pocket transistor I keep going under my pillow for company to beat time to my night dreams. Aunt V says it's bad for the head.

Bad for the head, she said to mom, to sleep with the radio on. Static, congressional investigations and body counts: it's unhealthy fare for an adolescent. Now if she tuned in on Vivaldi or Verdi it would be a horse of a different feather, but no, she gorges herself on the popular junk, candy, cookie & cake mix commercials when her mind should be on her diet to lose weight. Tell her to switch it off, J. You are her mother.

(Yes tell me, mother, smother me with a bear hug. Confiscate my little transistor: Smash it against the mirror. But kiss me good night.)

For crying out, V! Leave her alone.

Under my pillow the newscaster counts out the mangled bodies between two soul hits. THE POLITICS OF NEC-ROPHILIA HAVE HIT ROCK BOTTOM. THIS IS A PAID ANNOUNCEMENT. An air-raid siren has gone off under my pillow. He tells me to ignore the blast. THIS IS ONLY A TEST.

A test, how can he be sure it is not the real thing? Mom said the test tube was not the real thing, and Aunt V said that was what made it ideal, and though there were other methods to give them a baby—a date with a sailor on shore leave for instance, or with the adoption center, to name two possibilities out of a thousand—the tube seemed still the most desirable to her, the most discreet. No strings attached. No danger of a law suit or blackmail. Easy as mom's apple pie.

BINGO

Aunt V sighed, ah, if only we could make a baby without any male factor or substance intruding. You'd think that in our space age that shouldn't be hard. Science is stranger than fiction and in the labs and labor camps they're hard at work on self-fertilization, I saw a cut version of it on TV. Oh my Jay Boy (pressing mom to her bosom) it's I who should be carrying our child, look at my sturdy pelvis, feel my broad flanks. I could have had a baker's dozen if that woman-hating butcher Dr. X hadn't robbed me of my tubes in Aspen. Ah well, the mischief has been done and you will have to carry the little stranger for both of us. It only takes nine months.

Nine months to make a B or me. But I wasn't really the issue. The idea was the issue.

Nine months? Mom stared as though she hadn't known. Amen. She shut her eyes and hooked her thumbs into the belt of her faded, old dungarees.

Give a little take a little, said Aunt V. A child will keep you from drifting. You need an anchor, believe you me. I'm quoting my therapist.

Mom's eyes remained shut, she said, sure, hang a brat around my neck to keep me, no, not on the straight, though sure as hell on the narrow. And then she asked Aunt V to get lost.

But Aunt V never got lost. It was always mom who got lost, who would vanish from the house at the oddest times. I've lost her! Where is she? Aunt V would cry as she'd come home from her real estate office after a rough day of selling & buying. Where are you, J! she'd call, her voice flying out the window into the alley and down the waterfront past huddled, secret lights of piers and bars. Can you hear me, J? she'd call as she would search all over the house and even through the deacon's chest under the stairs as though mom were a ring Aunt V had mislaid. How had her J got lost, where or to whom, to what? When would she be back, if ever? In what condition? How hard would Aunt V have to scrub her mate to get the tar off that long, downy back?

But even when mom was present she often seemed absent, lost in a world of her own, and how grateful Aunt V had been when mom had said yes to the test tube for the sake of peace or for my sake. Once I was born there would be no more drifting, Aunt V had supposed, folding her into leather-sheathed arms at the reception desk of the Hospital of the Holy Sepulcher. Courage, mon vieux, I'll be right by your side to hold your hand.

But only patients were allowed behind the mysterious screen, and the attending M.D. hairy and male, no doubt a Russian type, kicked her out into the corridor.

Of course the brute was after J as should be clear to an unborn child, Aunt V insisted. Why else should he be substituting for the woman doctor whom she had handpicked to do the job? It was a plot.

Aunt V was pacing the corridor in her high boots, her face paler than pale under the brush-on powder called blushing rose. What was that hairy beast up to behind the screen? Her heels were striking the terrazzo up and down the evil corridor. She meant to phone her therapist or the police. But every public phone was out of order.

You'd think her girlfriend was having a baby, one nurse's aid mouthed to another through Danish pastry.

Aunt V, addressing an empty wheelchair, confessed she was having kittens.

I blew it, mom confessed with hangdog air a month or so after Aunt V's trial at the Holy Sepulcher.

He blew it! she screamed, threatening to sue the doctor for malpractice.

The time, the labor, the money she had wasted to prepare for my arrival. For I was to be welcomed like royalty, and was not J her prince, her royal master? She had spent a small fortune fixing up a nursery for me with mockup space men and genuine antiques from Spain, including a cradle certified to have been slept in by the infant Isabel and guaranteed to last for a year or your money refunded. Other certified antiques or rejects from the Smithsonian. Something old, something new, something blue. She was praying for a boy, little boy blue to jump out of mom's boy loins, dressed for the hunt and blowing his horn in the meadows. Mom could not have cared less what sex I was. But Aunt V wanted a boy for the sake of a more balanced family life, and she had purchased tons of boy toys, erectors, tractor, defectors, battle ships too, and the original Trojan horse from Bloomingdales. My nursery walls were in a blue swoon, waiting for me to arrive. But I never came.

Are you sure, J? Aunt V demanded, kneeling down in front of mom in that blue nursery in the blue morning and pressing an ear to mom's flat belly for a sign of life from me. She thought she heard something stir ever so faintly in her love's dark womb. But mom, crestfallen, shook her head no, sorry, there's nothing there, babe, just too much booze, gin and tonic.

For a short interlude she had been on the wagon for my

sake, but now that she found herself still without me, she had fallen off it again with a loud bang, smashing things and cursing and fighting Aunt V, though she wasn't any longer fighting me or the idea, she was beginning to want me almost as badly as Aunt V wanted me or worse, and she was ready, she said, to try anything, even sexual intercourse with a male partner.

Aunt V, biting her lips, thought it unnecessary to go to quite such extremes.

Don't let's jump overboard, J-J, let's not do anything rash you'd later regret. The tube is still our best bet, and I have arranged for a woman to woman talk with our very own Dr. H over drinks this afternoon in the garden.

Over drinks. Not to watch the ball game. The garden, yes, that's what she still calls our backyard with the stunted willow tree and the plastic tulips and roses in the ankle deep city soot. Nothing will grow in that yard except the soot. Once a dandelion appeared in a crack in the cement. It was like a miracle and none of the wild flowers in the hills in the country where we'd go weekends to meet the girls and granny-anny ever looked so wild and bright as did the stray little dandelion down there in the sooty backyard.

The sun was trying to cut through the soot when V & J sat down with Dr. H in the cast iron chairs, for free professional advice under the nothing willow. Patience. Rome wasn't built in a day, said the Frau Doktor, patting now V's hand, now J's. Don't blame yourself, girls, keep trying, I'm sorry I wasn't able to attend to the matter myself at the Holy Sepulcher, but I was down at the time with a still unidentified virus.

A frustrated bee, hunting in vain for nectar, came buzzing out of a plastic tulip. (No pollen on the breeches of that poor buzzer, observed Dr. H with a professional twinkle.) It's my contention, she went on, holding out the cocktail glass for another drop, that J's potential hasn't been aroused sufficiently. It's up to you to arouse it, she lectured Aunt V who was busily taking notes on a yellow scratch pad while mom, sullen and bleary-eyed, was staring through the gin at nothing.

Plan, structure, don't leave anything to chance, the doctor continued, retrieving the olive with two scrubbed, spatular fingers. Put the erogenous zones to their proper use with foresight and patience. Observe the lunar calendar, the phases, the curse of the moon; the bloody mucosal expulsions of monstrous menses. Now girls, may I use your phone? I must call my answering service, though I doubt that they will answer the phone.

Maternal and rotund, all smiles and dimples, doc has ground out her little cigar and bounced to her feet. My, my, what clever gardeners you are, she marvels with that merry old twinkle as she sniffs at a plastic American Beauty. Delicious fragrance. Tut tut, sisters. Do your job.

They followed doctor's orders and loved with an eye on the moon. They chalked off the days in the moon or the mirror and returned to The Holy Sepulcher for another shot at motherhood. No one can say I wasn't a wanted baby. They wanted me in the worst possible way. But again they missed, the womb stayed shut, double locked in secret self love.

No dice.

My bloody friend is here, god damn, said mom, slamming the toilet lid shut.

Who is here? Aunt V asks, not being on to J's girl talk from the old JHS days.

Nobody's here. The bloody flag is out. Find me a cunt rag.

Oh curse of womanhood. Woman hamstrung by the mandala, the mystic circle.

Will their union ever be blessed?

Aunt V, avidly licking a sheet of triple value trading stamps for redemption, pleads with mom to have another crack at the tube. Please, love . . .Will you do it? For me?

But mom, who has been drinking steadily since breakfast, has passed out on the floor by the cold fireplace.

What next, I wonder did it occur to them that they might send for me at the nearest mail order orphanage of their choice? Tax-deductible tots, prefabricated, ready-to-wear, are bawling their lungs out for a chance in the American family unit. Fill in your security number and state your first and second choice re color & greed. The black supply exceeds the white demand, my transistor says under my pillow in the black rain. LADIES & GENTLEMEN I GIVE YOU THE NATIONAL ANTHEM.

Two stations interfering with the night rain, GRAB IT AS LONG AS IT LASTS. DELIVERY FREE. Three stations: from the talking room below the voices rise again, brief and succinct:

Motherhood is born of sweat.

Of shit.

There is a report like a muffled gunshot and I wonder does it come from the pier. But perhaps it comes from the fire they keep going in the talking room to draw the dampness out of the old walls. They have thrown another log on the fire and now Aunt V is working the bellows, furiously; as mom says, you had your tongue hanging out, drooling after the real thing, the home-baked loaf out of my oven, but you don't know real from false, you are the last to know, for all your hours on the inflatable couch with your analyst.

The fire crackles, sputters, the fresh log sends off a series of tiny explosions into the night as they loll on their bellies on the big mama bear rug. Nothing in my oven, says mom, and I wonder what oven was I shoved into or out of, or did I join them ready-made.

B IS A TEST TUBE BABY, I read on the smeared wall of the women's toilet in Wash Sq Park. I didn't read the other graffitti, only the one about me or the mayor, it was written with a sky-blue eye liner in block letters that were leaning backwards with the wind. Those public toilets have a strange smell sometimes of lilacs. This was in the spring when everything smells of piss & pot & grass. But the lilac privy smell goes to your head and starts you flying. I took my magic marker out and wrote on the wall above me BARNUM & BAILEY BACH & BRAHMS & BAZOOKA & BLACK MARIA. Each one a test tube B. As I was doing my graffitti a little three year old came in and crapped right at my feet.

But it's the scent of lilacs that gives me a high. I've dusted some of it on my pillow from mom's after-shave talcum powder called Mayflower. Sometimes she dusts it on her armpits, although she never shaves. Aunt V shaves. Her armpits and crotch look like plucked chickens. But mom's are grown over with silky weeds. The weeds were aquiver as she raised her arms high in the three way mirror in the master or mistress bedroom where they both sleep. I saw them standing naked in the mirror. Aunt V was kissing mom's armpits in the lilac colored dusk in the mirror. I watched, her thumb curved upwards and slowly ran down mom's long spine.

Mom's face was talcum white. She kissed the mirror. Her body started to shake. The vanity table, shaped like a giant kidney, began to shake and the musical powder box toppled, it blew its lid and crashed to the floor to the tune of home on the range.

Oh give me a home. The tinkle survived the crash. The talcum powder made a blizzard. They giggled like kids.

The buff-a-loo is in the zoo, mom sang. They were standing belly to belly in the swirling snow, their nipples touching in the man-sized mirror. I ran downstairs to the kitchen and banged a spoon against the pots and pans. Doubletime I beat out the tune OH GIVE ME loud enough to beat hell. Flo came rushing up from the basement and grabbed the spoon from me and cried, will you shut your mouth, and she made as though she was going to spank me. I told her to spank me please, but she said, sorry, she had no license, Aunt V had warned her that nobody black or white was to raise a hand against me. Flo was black. She said, you'll never know how lucky you are to have that nice white lady protect you. But she said it with the oddest smile. I started to cry and for a while she let me sit on her lap and cry against her white uniform. Then she asked me to get up and wipe my face. She said, I'm not your big fat mammy. Go brush your hair, it's kinky like a nigger's I swear.

I sat down on the deacon's chest under the stairs and

brushed my hair until the sparks were flying. The ceiling light came on yellow. Mom and Aunt V were coming down the stairs together arm in arm, both of them dressed to kill for an opening night of King Lear or the Royal Ballet. Their look-alike dead white gowns reached down to their heels, and each had one shoulder bare and one feathered. Oops, said mom, tripping over the hem of her long gown. Aunt V caught her by the feathers and helped her round the tricky curve of the old stairway. My hair was crackling with the sparks. But they did not see me. They were passing the swinging hall mirror between the two antlers.

Tonight we are twins, vestal virgin sisters of Rome, sang Aunt V. Look. Aren't we gorgeous? Two highpriestesses.

Two highclass whores, said mom. Oops.

They passed from one mirror into another. Mom was slouching damp and limp behind the collapsible bar inside the closet lined with amber mirrors. She was drinking from the bottle (just one more snort, V) while Aunt V, still erect and trim in her lily white glitter gown, but with her smile slowly fading, was pointing at the sweetheart watch on her bosom. Darling, it is past curtain time. The show is nearly over, darling. Hadn't you better put down that bottle so we can leave in time for the last act?

What for? Mom shrugs her shoulders in seven mirrors. They have missed other shows before, they both know that, and the only show they'll never be too late for is right here in this house with its countless echoes, mirrors: mirrors flecked and warped with age, or broken, or newly replaced, with the glazier's label still glued to them or pasted over with last year's Valentines, lipstick red hearts, V&J's. The house is a maze of mirrors. You run into yourself at every turn.

There's no escape, and each time it is a different B I see because it is a different moment or mirror. Yesterday I saw a monster stare at me. I try not to look. I sleep.

The night is a black mirror. The little transistor is crackling in my hair. The fire crackles in the talking room as I try to remember how often I saw them through the mirror dressed in look alike white, Jeronima Veronica, two convent sisters. Was mom in white when she went down the waterfront to pick up a sailor and get herself big with me? More likely she was in black, or in her washed-out-hip-hugger J-jeans, the kind she still wears, the kind she wore when Aunt V first caught an eyeful of her at BANGS, friendly neighborhood bar for mothers and sisters. Mom had on a sweat shirt three sizes too big and with the owner's name written into the neckband in indelible ink: Oliver Bull. That name Aunt V learned before she learned mom's. For they had barely met, and she was tentatively breathing down mom's back when the name jumped up at her and stopped her cold in her tracks. Who was this Bull? She did not believe that he was an older brother. And so she confiscated the shirt and stepped on it and then she burned it.

But that was after the ball, after they had discovered each other amid the sleazy velvet drapes and plaster nymphs at BANGS and had retired to mom's cheap hotel room.

Good bye and good riddance, Oliver Bull! V cried, shoving the offensive shirt into the incinerator down the hall while mom was sleeping off her sins or sorrows in the broken-down bed.

The past had gone up in flames, Aunt V often said. Why

must it resurrect itself? Why must some clumsy bull always burst into their china shop and step on all their values, all her china? She more than any woman on earth had wanted to see a child in the house to hold the family together; but not at the expense of human decency. There was a limit even to her tolerance, she warned, and it made her sick to the heart that her J of all J's should spread her legs for some hairy, foul-smelling brute when there were less degrading methods of conception to be considered, as there were more ways than one to skin a cat, Aunt V supposed, and she for one had settled for adoption. She had scratched the idea that J should be the child's natural mother, for what, she demanded, breathing desperate and deep, did the word natural mean, and wasn't mother nature herself unnatural, playing, as she did, fast and loose with her own children?

Yes, she had been ready to cast her ballot for adoption. To offer a happy home to a homeless child would serve both them and the community. And service to the community had always been high on her list, Aunt V pointed out. If they adopted me they would be killing two birds with one stone, and it seemed perverse of J, to say the least, that she should suddenly insist she'd either have to get pregnant herself or chuck the whole project. What was behind this sudden reversal? Aunt V asked, her eyelid twitching. Was her partner hoping to prove to herself that she was after all a woman? Surely, said Aunt V with some derision, it was a little too late in the game for *that*!

But in their game it always was too late, she feared, and she knew she'd either have to give in to mom and take the blame and the abuses afterwards as usual, or watch mom leave the house for good as indeed she seemed to be leaving it anyway all the time, Aunt V remembered, sniffing, fidgeting with the door lock.

All right, J. Do what you must. But get it done and over with. No hanky-panky. No encores—I am warning you now. One quick go. Pick-ups anonymous. Then home, James. Did you hear me? HOME TO BIG SISTER.

So off to THE SEVEN BROTHERS, a low class no class public bar, though only a short walk from our own, private house. Aunt V might have felt safer, for reasons of personal hygiene, she said, if mom had chosen a nice cocktail lounge in midtown Manhattan. But mom said, go jump in the Hudson, I'm calling the shots, you can get the clap from an adman just as easy as from a seaman, so get off my back.

The agonies I endured! I hear Aunt V say to mom through the river mud of a thousand nights. On broken heels I paced outside The Seven Brothers. My feet were killing me. I almost fell into a manhole. I almost was mugged by a dyke. The sweetheart watch stopped on my bosom, the city went black, and from every blind alley I heard your call for help, I saw you with your throat slashed in every gutter, and through how many gutters, my love, did you roll that awful night of my golgotha?

There would be other golgothas. But the first was sure to be the worst, the longest. That long night had seemed endless. Sometimes she thought it was still going on. Sometimes she felt as though she never had stopped pacing outside that dreadful bar where her love had been downing drink after drink, her head tilted backward, her kohled eyes shut tight as she had been laughing, laughing at God knows what stupid joke. Never had she laughed so hard at home. Only seconds had passed since she had flopped down on the bar stool and flashed the V sign through the fly-specked window across the sun kissed beer ad, Milwaukee's bluest. And already a sailor had jumped from the shadows and slipped his hand under the seat of her pants.

Chin pressed into the silver fox collar, Aunt V paced, prayed—how long o lady love my lord how long—while a juke box or Hammond organ made hallowed sounds. World without end. When would the jackass from the Destroyer Wisconsin get his fat ass off the bar stool, his fat paw off J, and disappear with her no matter where to as long as he shipped her home fast, back to big sister?

Big sister, poor Veronica, where is your sweat cloth? Her sweat is running hot and cold. Time's running out. She peers through silver fox whiskers and sees the big-knuckled hand on little sister's brown waist, summer tan they both so tenderly tended in granny-anny's pasture in the hills. Brown you are comelier, my love. Dark you are fairest. Color slide memories of J's glistening body adrift upon a yellow tide of buttercups flash on and off in her head in rapid succession. And now she feels the old jealousy tear through her guts and burn her abdomen until she reels and, doubles up at the curb. Lay off my tomboy! Don't touch her! Just make her big. We want a baby doll for Christmas, daddy.

But dad had already blacked out in the sawdust, and the game had to be played over again—through how many unspeakable nights? She had lost count. Each night was first night, she said, and by now she was certain, she swore, that J was doing it for kicks, that she got a kick out of her role and maybe even out of her roommate's agonies. Half the crew of the destroyer Wisconsin must have sailed through mom's port, and still she wasn't pregnant with me. It's obvious, screamed Aunt V, that the only mother you'll ever be is to the navy.

If J really wanted to become a mother, would she get herself mixed up in those tavern brawls with the whores? Would she be taking the whores to bed if she were serious?

Aunt V screamed in a shriller tone. For half the time she'd lose her sailor somewhere between here and Fulton, and wake up the next morning in a strange hotel room in bed with a whore. Not even Aunt V, for all her solicitude, could be expected to walk guard every night in front of a cheap waterfront bar where no decent woman should ever be seen alone. And how many times hadn't she been propositioned in the street by those very same sailors who'd later proposition J, she might say, hoping to make her jealous.

I may not be the youngest anymore, said Aunt V with a flip of the hip, but I am still as attractive to the opposite sex as I was when I married my first X.

But mom merely spit over her shoulder and walked off with that peculiar walk of hers which resembled more and more an old salt's on shore leave.

Poor Aunt V, she could not turn the tide, much though she paced the waterfront, trying, she said, to be her brother's keeper. There always came the moment when the iron shutter went down and she was left with nothing except an empty bed at home and a fantasy parade of rivals crowding her night. Those ghostly rivals: she said they were more real than the real ones she'd watch through a bullet hole in the tavern window, across Milwaukee's bluest beer ad lake. She never knew how J would be winding up the night, or whether she would ever come back to her. She had agreed to lend mom out for a few hours. But the few hours would stretch into days and nights. For mom had no watch.

Once a hooker always a hooker, Aunt V said when she thought she could bear it no more, those excruciating jealousy pains in her abdomen, those ghostly visitations when, alone in the giant, custom-made bed, she'd imagine mom lying with all the seamen, and their sweethearts, and their mothers too. There was nothing she, Aunt V, did not imagine. And had not mom balled an Eskimo on an Arctic slope, under a blanket?

You were hustling in Fairbanks, Alaska. I've checked your police record all over the U.S.A. And what, if I may ask, were you up to that night at BANGS in the ladies room? (No, BANGS don't have a men's room, I grant you that.) I pulled you out of the gutter and gave you all I have, myself, my money. And how do you repay me? You have no respect or love for anyone, not for me and not for yourself. You are set on destroying yourself and everything with it, including me, so go ahead, what are you waiting for! Kill me!

Kill her with what—her nylon hose? Her gun? I wonder where she keeps her gun, in which secret drawer of my blue nursery where I never slept.

Kill me! Aunt V tears her blazer open. The buttons are flying. She grabs the carving knife and offers it to mom to stab her with and then she grabs her left breast and offers that so she should be stabbed through the heart. But mom is weak and blue after many nights of drifting. Mom is drained and lost, a lost swimmer. She gropes for Aunt V and hangs on to her neck as to a single pole in a deep lake. She hangs on, sobbing, begging: Save me, V. Don't let me drown. Save me, sister.

Mom drowning in the flooded river mud night after night. I tried to drown myself in the swimming pool Aunt V has built on her land in the hills. It is V-shaped and fed by a brook, and you can see it from far away, that bright blue triangle flung against the white bloom of the apple orchard. Aunt V calls the old farm her retreat or her nest and the

girls who come trooping there weekends call it SAPPHO'S
SILO. But to me it will always be granny-anny's place and
nothing else. I pinched my nose and let myself drop into the
pool in my white night shirt, with flowers in my hair like
Ophelia. The pool went deep and blue, but I stayed up. My
shirt was billowing above me like a sail. I couldn't swim, and
yet I couldn't sink. Was it my fat that kept me from going
under? Eyes shut I floated on my back into the sun.

Hush, said Aunt V, drying my hair with a towel and
slapping caramels into my mouth to prevent me from hollering murder. Your granny-anny died a natural death as
you well know. We all do miss her, we miss her cooking,
those oodles of noodles and strudels, though don't forget
how her old world peasant cuisine has ruined your figure.

I asked, who killed her? My wet night shirt or Ophelia's
had dried in the sun. Still I felt cold.

Killed? Good lord, child, what tripe! Mother passed away
at—was she ninety? A remarkable woman, although a little
queer toward the end. But then, senility will come to most of
us in one form or another. I loved and honored my mother,
and of course I supported her as I seem to be supporting
just about everybody's mother, including yours. Now hush.
As soon as we get back to the city we'll get you started on a
sensible diet. Once we have made you lose that extra poun-
dage, you'll feel like a new B.

Another caramel. I suck and sulk. The caramels taste of
sand. Aunt V's face is like sand under the wide straw hat.
Beechnuts come raining down on us. We are sitting under
the same big tree where granny-anny used to tell me a sad
old world story about a little girl whose best friend, a toad,
was killed by a careless mother. Granny-anny said never to
kill a toad as they were said to bring luck. But if you touched
a toad even with your little finger you would get warts.

Granny-anny took a knitting needle and scratched my name into the bark of the tree in Croatian for no other reason than that I asked her to do it. There were warts on the back of her hand.

You must learn to grow up, says Aunt V. When I was your age I had to earn money. Not that I believe a girl of 13 needs to make a living, and in fact I trust you will concentrate on an education for which I am more than willing to pay. But perhaps you have been living too sheltered a life, with me and mom and Flo protecting you from reality. Ah, here comes my buzzard! I want him in the picture.

Summer sunday sketcher V has picked up a new pencil. The pages of her sketchbook teem with weathercocks and barns and carpentry gothic—tidy little churches with no altar to kneel at. Soon she will add a few Greek windmills and fishing boats. She is planning to take mom away from the temptations of the city to go island hopping in the Aegean Sea. Don't get yourself sick while we are gone, she says, remembering no doubt the last time they left me behind when I came down with a bad case of the mumps, and Flo was trying to phone them in Marrakesh but couldn't get the N. Y. operator. What will I be sick with this time? I can't decide.

The buzzard! Aunt V is squinting upwards through one eye as she measures the sky with a pencil. But the buzzard has flown out of sight before she could trap him between two identical cloudlets above our old roofless barn.

Ah well, there will be other birds to sketch. Aunt V drops the sketchbook onto the grass and gingerly touches a bruise on her well-exercised leg. I'll bring you back, she says, a beautiful doll, perhaps a genuine antique to help the economy. I know you'd rather see us stay, but your mother has been indulging a bit too much, and the only way we can get her to dry up is to keep her busy traveling, provided we'll get her away from the city. I hope we can, she is under great emotional strain, good god, the other night she beat me up till I was black and blue all over the jolly landscape beyond the delta. I don't mind telling this to you or anyone else. Our group encounter therapist has urged us to let everything come out. Talk, talk, no matter who listens, he's told us. Remove the stopper and let the juice gush out or the old bottle is sure to burst.

Aunt V is talking rapidly, now stroking her bare legs, now fiddling with the red tassels that hang from her blouse. A faded old peasant blouse embroidered in the wild Croatian hills by children and old women, by granny-anny perhaps, long ago.

Two butterflies alight on the open sketchbook in the grass and paint a beautiful picture, deep orange and yellow. The sun is riding the crest of the hill. Pull out that stopper! Was she wrong divorcing Jock, her second husband? she asks, shading her eyes to look at a distant flag pole. Was she wrong trading one J for another J?

I blink against the sun and ask, who was he? Was he a he, was he a she? Pull out the stopper.

What a child you still are! Aunt V marvels and she blows me a kiss. I'm as straight as the next guy, not even bilingual, or so I have been assured by my guru. My marriage could have been successful if that woman-hating doctor hadn't removed my procreant organs. I ask you, B: why did Jock permit it, unless he too wanted to see me castrated? Of course Jock never really loved me. He was like Ludwig V B, in love with his piano and with his nephew. When I was under the knife, he was at his ninth symphony, though unlike the deaf titan he never sold a single composition, and it was left to me to bring home the bacon and pay off his nephew, and the piano tuner too.

Aunt V rolls her eyes. Penis envy: that was what bugged her Jock. He was much weaker, much less resourceful than she was, and so he envied her her penis, and whether or not she had one had nothing whatever to do with the price of beans.

Am I talking over your head, B?

You are and you aren't, I say. The butterflies have taken off, orange and yellow. High overhead a jet cuts a silver arrow into the blue. I throw myself into the fat grass and let myself roll down the hill happy and faster than you could say Jock, J or Jesus. The trees are flying upside down in the air. I travel fast and laugh. Aunt V has vanished. Down I roll through the tumbleweeds into the fog of the valley into the night.

I broke my ass for you, mom says to Aunt V (their voices seeping from the Pullman Parlor talking room through wads of horse hair, broken bottles, mirrors). The whole crew from the skipper down to the sweeper were lining up to plant their prick into my piece of sod. Fuck you and your tax deductible womb, I bet you your bottom dollar you sold it for a good price to a medical school. I loathe you for using me as your substitute belly, and don't you hush me, the brat was your idea and yours alone.

Hush, J! What does it matter whose idea? I worship you. For you I would do anything, even cut off my ear like Vincent V G.

OK. Cut off your clit.

Mom burning with gin, belching with tonic. I used to call it quinine bubble water. They would have fed it to me as a baby to keep me from bawling my lungs out if Aunt V hadn't learned from the baby book that gin would stunt my growth. So I grew faster and bigger than any of them—too big for their comfort. I eat and eat. Last night I dreamed I ate up my tongue. It tasted of chocolates.

CRASH. A bottle has shattered against a mirror. Mom, roaring drunk, tears through the talking room Aunt V has fitted with the overstuffed lounge chairs, draperies and special mirrors from President Garfield's train—the one he never got to board. BANG. I'm sitting up in bed, not scared at all. Dead soldiers are playing the bugle on my transistor. Let mom tear the roof down. I wait.

The roof sits tight. It may take a bomb to smash it. The house is built of solid brick, with the brass knocker on the front door wrought in the shape of the American eagle. Aunt V keeps the bird polished. She says she is proud of him, she is proud to be a solid first generation non-degenerate American citizen who generously gives to the LOST CHILDREN'S FUND and related causes. She gives as much and often as traffic will bear, especially when the charity is sponsored by our local police. She supports them and they support her in turn. Those boys at the precinct really watch out for her like so many brothers which is a good thing, she says, what with the anti-social elements prowling about—prostitutes, pimps, narcotics and seamen too drunk to remember which ship they jumped.

The ships: I hear them blow their horns high and low through the night. I see the river in the sky, at night. Daytimes I must climb to the roof to see it. Then it seems to flow and roar right under me. Then the house becomes my ship and I shout into the wind, into the smell of the ocean. But down at ground level, in that little old alley where we live next to a condemned, boarded-up house, everything smells of piss.

We all complain of the smell. Even Aunt V screws up her face and holds her nose, overcome; until she remembers that it isn't all that bad. It could be worse. Think positive, sisters! At least the urinal stink cancels out the stink of the countless trucks which belch up enough filth and noise to poison eternity. Besides, let's not forget, girls, that ours is one of the few homes left in the city which hasn't yet been burglarized, or shot at, or burned to the ground. No stranger would guess we had any riches worth stealing, the way we sit squeezed in among abandoned warehouses, condemned buildings, all of which are owned by V V REALTIES INC—a most valuable land investment, Aunt V says with a modest lowering of her eyes. We are camouflaged by relics of the past—the skeleton of a factory, the rusted, gutted hulk of a ship—and no one would expect to find a private home in such surroundings. Indeed, few outsiders are aware that our alley exists at all, and those who happen to run into it, don't bother to stop, except to urinate by our steps. Then they move on. We have a safe little nest, Aunt V says with a bright smile.

You piss me off, says mom, munching on an apple and spitting the seeds with amazing precision across the length of the table and into a tall Chinese vase. The mere mentioning of a nest upsets her, and Aunt V talks about nests all the time, at home and at her office and on the radio—HOW BEST TO INVEST IN A NEST—the jingle squeals in my transistor like a litter of new-born rats. Aunt V is convinced that woman was born with the nesting instinct built into her like a bed is built into those convertible sofas. It was her built-in convertible nesting instinct which made her go into real estate after a first divorce and a second World War, on

V or J Day, she says, when property was to be had dirt cheap for cash if you had it, she did, she bought up rows of broken down brownstones for nothing and made them over into cozy nests to sell or rent though not for peanuts. She made a bundle. Of course the improvements cost her a pretty penny, as some of the houses had been in such a state of total neglect, even the rats had begun to pack up and move out.

Sure, mom says, spitting apple seeds, one, two, three, four, into the vase. You kicked the tenants out and so the rats moved out. Old rat exterminator V. You made gold out of rat shit.

Your mom is talking through her head, Aunt V says to me. Your mom never saw a rat until she ran away from a lovely home to haunt the waterfront bars. She is a dropout from suburbia, though hearing her talk it's hard to believe that her daddy has a doctorate in education and her mummy a certificate to teach speech. I never had your advantages, she continues, turning her eyes back on mom. I was raised in poverty, and every cent you are spending I've labored for. What I earned I earned by the sweat of my brow and with a short term loan from Jock, I mean Jake, my first X and indeed my first J as well.

Your first and last, mom says with a vacuous stare.

Aunt V pours water into her wine, sipping, frowning as she asks what's wrong with grabbing up run-down property cheap and transforming old tenements into air-conditioned nests with sunshine and the like for those who can afford it? Of course everybody ought to have some sunshine within reason, but few can pay for it and she can only hope for better conditions. She has just accepted the chairwoman ship of the neighborhood improvement committee to decorate the garbage cans and keep the drunks out of the vest-pocket parks.

I don't deny that I feathered my own nest, says Aunt V, reaching down the neck of her see-through blouse where one of mom's apple seeds must have gone astray after all. But if I didn't have a head for business, where would this family be?

Boo, mom says in such a low and faraway voice, I almost think it's someone else talking inside her belly. Her eyes are distant too, they have the owl look, as if a second lid had gone down over the eye like a thin film. You still see her pupils the color of dark honey under the film and she isn't looking at Aunt V who is looking down her own blouse. Mom is looking across the table at the big fat-bellied Chinese vase which seems forever on the verge of toppling and breaking. Boo, says the voice out of mom's belly. She has dropped the stem which is all that's left of the apple. She has scraped her chair back and is sleepwalking toward the vase, and I wait for her to pick it up and smash it.

But no, she simply stands there and stares at it as though she never saw it before and maybe she never did see it until this moment, her eyes are different from other eyes. She stands poised on the balls of her feet which are always grimy like mine. She shakes her head in wonderment and with her thumb she traces the landscape that's painted across the vase gray and white. (The other thumb she keeps hooked into the nail-studded leather belt of her old dungarees.) She traces three clouds and then one gray cliff and then the little old man who is squatting beneath, trying to fish with a long fishing pole although there are no fish. There is no water.

But now the sun comes in from the talking room and bounces off a mirror so that the little old man on the vase is suddenly fishing in ripples of water. Mom is floating in the mirror in the water very still. I float alongside her and our arms touch under the water.

I wonder if I haven't been had, says Aunt V who is aware of nothing except the vase, its actual value, and whether it's genuine ming or a fabulous fake as GG insists. She bought it with the provision that she could return it, but now it turns out that the dealer has skipped the country and she is stuck with what may well be a fake, at least according to GG who owns an art shop called INSTANT ANTIQUES FOR MEN on Christopher Boulevard.

Should she try to sell the vase? Perhaps the Metropolitan Museum would buy it, Aunt V says, digging into the low calorie mousse. The Metropolitan is full of fakes, if she is to believe GG, and why shouldn't she? He is an expert. Yes, maybe she'll try to pawn off the ming thing on the MM, let's hope at a profit, with GG as her middleman, she says, addressing the vase in that pool or puddle of sun where mom had been floating seconds before, though she has already vanished again as though for ever, has floated through the door and out of sight.

But it always does seem for ever, each time she vanishes from sight, although she rarely vanishes so quietly. There usually is a terrible battle first and at least one broken vase or mirror before mom slams the door behind her to leave Aunt V bereaved once again, forever. Then, desperate for company, she might try to phone GG or any other two letter fellows on whose sympathy she knows she can bank. The fellahs, she calls them. She says they are her friends in need, certain to take her side and never mom's when there has been domestic strife, as indeed there is most of the time, and even now in the black of night the battle is on.

Aunt V says the fellows make her feel like a real woman, especially after one of those screaming, nerve-shattering fights when her very womanhood has been shattered. None of the girls of her acquaintance could quite restore her femininity the way the fellows can restore it, the girls being too masculine, she fears, to identify with female complexities. But the fellows, they identify with her. They understand her. They bring her flowers—real flowers. They hug her, kiss her on the mouth and tell her how gorgeous she looks in her striped pj's and matching tortoise shell glasses, how chic, how grand.

They bring her sweetheart roses and dry her tears. (Don't cry, V. The bitch isn't worth it!) And if by chance they forgot to buy flowers, they'd simply pick a few of her own out of the vase for an improvised gift, and by God, she'd be so delighted, you never would believe that she had bought those carnations herself only that morning. She'd smile with tears in her eyes and thank them profusely. What counts, she'd say, is the idea. The idea.

The idea, she might say to me, is to have as many male visitors at the house as the traffic will bear. For what you need, my child, is a father image to help you grow up normal in a wholesome atmosphere of mixed sex.

And so, whenever they'd drop by for drinks, usually in the late afternoon, she'd call me on the intercom to hurry down and join the party. We'd hug and kiss, there always was much of that and they said I was pretty, and they brought me chocolates and told Aunt V not to worry about my weight as it was only baby fat and I was sure to outgrow it and grow into a gorgeous woman like herself.

They all came in doubles, GG, ZZ, DD, OO, like at a two
for one sale. I called them any name I pleased, but never
daddy, and each looked new to me each time, with different
hair or teeth or eyes. It mixed up my head. They'd let me
mix a pitcher of dry martinis—the merest whiff of V, they'd
sing through a patchquilt of sun and shadows as they would
sit in the sooty yard around the mirror top table among the
plastic zinnias. They liked the table, but not the flowers.
Why not grow real ones? they might ask, their mirrored
faces in the table fusing yellow and round like one big
sunflower.

I've tried to grow real ones, Aunt V might sigh. But
everything dies here in the city, and even out in the country
my flowers won't come out the way they used to when
mother was still alive.

But granny-anny never died, I'd think as I would pass the
drinks, with mom sneering down at us from an upstairs
window—the window of my old nursery? I'd pass the carrot
sticks as she'd shout down that they were a bunch of free-
loading maggots or faggots. You goddamn mothers, buy
your own booze! she'd yell. Buy your own carrots! And
she'd slam the window shut hard enough to break the
panes. There always was broken window glass in our yard.

They did not defend themselves. They chose to ignore
her. But when she was out of sight as she usually was, then
they would go to work on her and call her all kinds of
names, bitch, butch, or butcher dyke or bull, and how, they
cried, could wise and beautiful V ever have permitted that
nasty hustler to hook her?

I love her! I've lost her! Aunt V would sob as a shower of
broken glass would rain down from my old nursery window. And the fellows, handing her paper tissues, pocket
handkerchiefs and cocktail napkins to mop up her tears

would say, alas, if only the creature would get lost, only she never would, she'd be back to take poor V for all she was worth which was plenty, she'd come stomping back to kick dear poor V out of her own nest.

But why? Why? Why? Aunt V would cry, flapping her wings like a flustered hen.

Because, they'd say, that's how they all are. She'll have you make the house over in her name, and then she'll throw you out like that. Finie la guerre.

I've heard it before. Mom is going to chase Aunt V out of her house. You'll be left without a roof over your head, they warn, as though they had forgotten how many other houses she owns. She starts to sob again. She too must have forgotten those other houses. I have forgotten them. I imagine Aunt V homeless, roofless, hatless in the downpour by the river. Now mom and I have the big house for ourselves. We have decided to sleep each night in a different room. But we like it best on the roof. There we sleep in sleeping bags. The roof is the deck of our ship.

Why? Why would she want to drive me out? Aunt V keeps asking.

Because. . . . they say and Aunt V puts a finger to her lips—hush! Not in front of the child!

The child . . .What is Aunt V afraid of? In my head I am not even there. In my head I am on the roof with mom. She is fast asleep in her old sleeping bag. It will be difficult to wake her up and I shall have to guard her with my life. I am watching out for both of us. The Milky Way makes a huge arch in the night sky. I'm standing guard.

The foghorn speaks low and dark. Down in the talking room Aunt V and mom are playing their favorite record.

BONNE NUIT CHERIE. Are they dancing to the record? Are they fighting?

BONNE NUIT CHERIE, it says on the back of the little jacket Aunt V sports in bed. A brief pink jacket which barely covers her navel, she likes to lounge about the house like that, the top of her dressed up, the bottom bare. She bought the jacket in France, at La Belle Helène in Paris. Paris is her wonderland, the Disney Land Amusement Park of all her dreams.

Bonne nuit, chérie, she sang, tucking me in and kissing me goodnight for mom. I asked her who owned the house, and she said I would as soon as I was of age, she was leaving everything she had to me and to my dear mother of course. Share and share alike: that, she said had always been her motto, except when it came to lovers.

You'll be well off once I am gone, she said, but promise me to finish your education. Don't be like your mother who dropped out of Junior High and consequently never learned to spell. She has brains, but no sitzfleisch—sitting flesh, roughly translated. I learned the word from a roommate who preceded J in the alphabet of my past. She was a deaf mute who mastered 15 languages but spoke not one—poor dear, though her manner was extremely aggressive, doubtless to compensate for her absolute silence. Ah well, she has her M.L and a husband in Hackensack. Men prefer their women dumb, you should have no problem finding a husband, what with your poise and complexion all dimples, no pimples. But first do get a college degree, please promise, though deep down in my heart I suspect that education and a career can wreck a woman's marriage or vice versa. Forget the rat race, stay home with the children, I say, and let your man provide for you. Men love to compete in the open market, that's why their life expectancy is lower than ours. They die early. I wish I'd had the good fortune to stick with my man. But then, I never had your kind of security. You'll make it as a wife and mother, eventually. But don't you throw yourself away on just anybody. You only have one hymen. Hold on to it. Don't imitate those dames who burn flag, bra & girdle. Burn up your calories instead. Exercise. Jog with J for god and country. And for god's sake learn not to shove food into your mouth all the time . . .

My mouth, she said, and all the time. But that was at a different time, in the country, before the big storm hit the hills and ripped the roof off the old barn Aunt V liked to sketch. The storm clouds came rolling in fast. The wind was whipping up the dust behind the grocery store, and through the wire fence, the dust, I saw a baby chick being pecked to death by the mother hen. I might have saved the chick. But I didn't dare climb over the barbed wire. The chick was dead and still the mother kept pecking away at it and clucking like all fury. She scared me to death.

Survival of the fittest, Olli said. He had jumped down from his dad's delivery truck and was creeping up from behind me the way he always does in those sneakers of his which are like mom's, dirty and full of holes. He said the chick didn't have a chinaman's chance. It came out of the egg with only one wing. It was a cripple.

He pinched me and off we ran, down the road together and behind the garbage dump into the bushes.

BONNE NUIT CHERIE for god and country. I didn't learn it from the birds and bees. I learned it from a good night book: FUN WITH MR. SPERM & MRS. OVUM. Picture fun with funny-faced blobs and blubbers. I wonder whose Mr. S shacked up with mom's Mrs. O, and how did she get pregnant with me at least three times over. I know she aborted me once. The next time I almost made it. But it was a still birth. I was born dead. That birth or death of mine shook her up worse than the others, I know, no matter how she would protest that she didn't want me or any brat, that I was Aunt V's idea.

I keep thinking of the baby corpse which once was me. If I knew where they put me away I'd visit my grave. But no one seems to know, not even black Flo although she has second sight and has been with us forever, having come with the house, says Aunt V. No use my asking mom about my grave. She pretends the still birth never happened. It so broke her up when it happened she locked herself into the rumpus room with a crate of gin. Aunt V had to call a locksmith to get her out.

Perhaps I have no grave. Perhaps they threw me into the fireplace. I've combed through the ashes. But I found nothing. Once I found a small chicken bone.

Like mom I'd rather forget. It's Aunt V who keeps harping on the still birth, asking why, why did it have to happen to *them*! Oh, that other time when her J had lost me after maybe two months, no one had been surprised, what with her drinking like a fish at BANGS and diving from a fire boat into the Hudson dead drunk, and riding the top of the garbage truck and the Ferris wheel on Coney Island. But the next, the crucial time when she had carried me for nine months she had been an angel. She had followed doctor's orders with a docility astonishing in one who was so rebellious by nature, so careless with her own body. She had quit smoking (except for an occasional pipe or cigar) and had sworn off hard liquor for the duration. She had drunk a quart of milk a day, though she had always loathed milk. No roaming through the bars. No unexplained absences. She had been in bed before midnight each single night.

Ah, those months were heaven, a second honeymoon, Aunt V recalls, slipping the wedding band off her finger and peering through it—at me? Never before or since, she says, were they so close to each other in body and spirit. There were no fights, no broken glasses or promises. Even my blue nursery which used to make her J boy sick to the stomach now filled her with joy. No morning sickness either, and oh, she looked so heavenly, her J with the swelling breasts and the swollen belly. She'd rock my empty cradle, humming BONNE NUIT CHERIE. She would diaper the plastic doll Aunt V had bought for her at Bloomingdales to practice on. Nine months of pure serenity. Nine months of peace. And why, dear god, did it have to end, why did fate have to play such a vicious trick on three innocents?

Three, says Aunt V, including me, and sometimes she says four, including Flo, maybe to show that we are all in it together regardless of color. Four victims, says Aunt V, opening her heart in the kitchen while Flo is washing the dishes before stacking them up in the portable dishwasher to be washed over again. Everything is done twice in this house. Everybody has a twin. Poor baby, Aunt V says, squeezing me tight to her chest. And all at once I think that perhaps it's me who is both victim number three and number four. I had a twin. It was born dead. But the other twin stayed alive for one day at least, and that twin was B, was me. For if I never was alive at mom's breast at least for a moment, why would she grieve over my death bad enough to lock herself into the poolroom with a crate of gin? No one would be that mushy, certainly not mom who calls Aunt V a sentimental ass for wearing a paper poppy on V day.

The fields of Flanders, says Aunt V to Flo. I saw them on a guided tour a year ago and I was shaken. Still our private tragedies shake us up so much worse than the historical disasters of war. Don't you agree?

Yes, ma'm, says Flo with a heavy stress on the *ma'm*, smiling, blinking as Aunt V jumps as though she had been hit in the stomach. How often must she beg Flo not to call her ma'm but to call her V, for god's sake? This wasn't a southern plantation. This was a progressive town house with the American eagle screwed to the front door.

Yes, ma'm, says Flo and again I wonder if she doesn't have the same contempt for Aunt V that she has for mom, though to mom she won't even speak. I think I am the only one in the house she doesn't despise. We talk, and when I get into the cooky jar she makes believe she is blind.

Steal away for Jesus. Flo and I hit it off from the start before I was born.

That still birth: what a tragic waste, says Aunt V. Where did we go wrong, Flo? I retained the most expensive obstetricians. The one who flew in from Zurich performed the autopsy . . . remember . . . something was terribly wrong with the central brain . . .

Aunt V is squeezing me tighter. I gasp for air. I try to bite her wrist to free myself while Flo says, yes, ma'm, yes, ma'm, in a cold monotone. No use, she says, crying over spilled milk.

Spilled mother milk?

It's always the children who have to bear the brunt, says Aunt V. Poor B, she says, unaware how I struggle in vain to get loose. Poor B. Her mother's refusal to admit it ever happened doesn't make it easier on the child. Small wonder she was so slow growing up.

Slow to walk and slow to talk. But I always was a fast eater. I licked my platter clean. I hollered for extras. Fat, lean: I gobbled it up.

Bulimia. A pathological craving for food. Her therapist is itching to treat me but I won't let him. I prefer to stuff myself. I knock myself out with goodies the way mom does with booze, and he'd be more than glad to treat her too, he'd willingly take on the whole gang of us, V&J&B at a reduced rate on his divan. But mom says hands off. She is no better than I, and it is sinful, says Aunt V, how we abuse ourselves in the eyes of god.

Yes, ma'm, says Flo. You do. **1903632**

Sinful, Aunt V says. Like B, J is an only child, they both are compensating for something that's lacking, maybe sibling rivalry, though in B's case it's also the Oedipus thing she is missing. No steady daddy. How can we make her eat less? Should we buy her a pet?

Buy her a pet and she'll eat that too, Flo says slowly with a slow derisive sneer for Aunt V.

And Aunt V, who has made it a rule never to contradict a black citizen as long as the issue doesn't involve money or politics, nods and says, yes, you may be right, still I believe it might be worth a try.

Not for the pet it won't be, says Flo. And then she laughs. It is a scary, rolling laughter like thunder. Her body which is almost as fat as mine begins to heave and shake and her flesh bursts through the seams of that uniform Aunt V makes her wear, a white, starched uniform designed not for a maid but for a nurse. A coffee mug has fallen off the hook and onto the tiled floor where it rolls unbroken. I have wrenched myself loose from the furious V-hug. My whole body aches. I start to bawl and hang my face into the cooky jar.

Bulimia, Aunt V says, is a peculiar disorder, involving more than food. Mental patients, prisoners and the like have been known to swallow any hardware they can get their hands on—nails, coffee spoons, razor blades, thumb tacks, etc. Of course the result may be illness or death. I heard that in one convict's stomach the surgeons found the key to his cell door. He had managed to steal it for his escape. But he couldn't resist swallowing it. What on earth did I do with my keys!

Aunt V is fumbling through her pockets. Her keys! She must have mislaid them again—but where? Surely she didn't swallow them, she says, trying to laugh into an uneasy silence, aware only now perhaps that Flo stopped her scary laughter minutes ago and is watching her with narrowed eyes. Those eyes are narrowed like an Indian's, and not a muscle moves in her face as she watches Aunt V.

Why do I always lose my keys? Aunt V says to no one. And then she adds with a forced smile, come now, Flo, you're teasing me, you don't seriously think B would kill her pet just to satisfy a craving for food! Though Aunt V isn't really saying this to Flo at all but into some kind of wilderness of her own making.

Flo doesn't reply. She stands with her arms crossed, immensely black in her white uniform in the white kitchen. She never blinks, she opens her mouth and moves her tongue very slowly in a wide circle over her wide lips. I see it from across the cooky jar—how Flo's tongue keeps sweeping around and around while she continues to watch Aunt V through those narrowed, unblinking eyes.

Neither one of them says a word. Aunt V stands as though hypnotized, with her back flat to the wall and her eyes held fast by Flo's eyes. Then she too opens her mouth and her tongue comes darting out of it like a gray mouse to sweep, like Flo's tongue, in that same slow circle over the thin, painted lips.

I stare. I too am hypnotized. But suddenly the clock in the

talking room strikes one and the spell is broken.

Really! This is obscene! Aunt V cries out. Her face is blotched. Her mouth is gray. Obscene! she cries, throwing her bejeweled hands over her mouth.

Yes, ma'm, Flo says simply. Her face is a blank mask. She has uncrossed her arms and bends over the sink as if nothing has happened. Nothing has happened, except an ice cold shiver inside me, all the way down my spine, my legs, my heels.

Obscene, how we allow her to stuff herself! cries Aunt V, leaping forward. There will be no more sweets in this house! she cries, tearing the cooky jar away from me and emptying it into the trash can. No more sweets! Is that understood, Flo?

Yes ma'm.

Aunt V is biting her lips. She walks out of the kitchen, dragging her feet as though she had suddenly aged a hundred years. Your uniform needs mending, Flo, she says weakly over her drooping shoulder. The seams are split. Then she shuffles on, mumbling to herself as she starts searching through the house for her keys.

Obscene, the way she licked her fat lips. Of course she did it to insult me, Aunt V says in the talking room to mom. Flo's walrus tongue—I couldn't begin to describe it . . .Huge, pink and slimy, oh my god . . .

Sounds yummy to me, says mom.

Try not to be vulgar, J. Think of your daughter.

You think of her, babe.

I swear, J, she hates my guts, I mean Flo does. The nightmares I've been having, you have no idea, her horrid tongue was all over and into me, it changed, Jesus, it became Jake or Jock, Jock's you know what . . .

Jock's cock. Go succotash, says mom. Wet dreams are not for nice little ladies.

Jock, Jake or Joke. I make my own wet dreams. Not that I have trouble holding my water. I can store it up like a desert camel. I wet my bed because I like to, I like the damp smelly warmth in my sheets.

The night's too long. Jock & Jake: They might be an ethnic policy expert team on my little transistor.

WHAT'S NEW WITH THEM, JAKE?
NOTHING GOOD, JOCK.
THAT'S THEIR PROBLEM, JAKE.

Jock-Jake: They might be one and the same person the way Aunt V mentions her 2 X's in 1 breath. What X smashed up his Stradivari? A racing car, believe me, not a violin. He raced it for kicks through the Painted Desert and crashed into an adobe schoolhouse. Nine little Indians dead. Whatever his name, Jake or Jock, he didn't even lose his driver's licence.

Kiss daddy, he said, stopping by the house on his way to Death Valley. He offered me his cheek. It smelled of bacon. He was stopping by to ask his X for a small loan, but she and mom were abroad, cruising through the Aegean. No bread, Flo said, go sell your superduper souped-up heap. He wouldn't even say goodbye to us, he was too angry, he took off in his Stradivari with a roar like a lion into the painted sunset sky.

He's not my dad, not by a long shot, though somebody must be, but who? Nobody tells me. It's like the still birth, they can't for the life of them figure what brought it about, and they no more would mention my dad than they'd mention the twins. It is all guesswork.

It is god's work, said granny-anny under the tree, and don't you ask too many questions. The child that asks one too many will have her hand grow out of her grave.

Stop it, mama, said Aunt V, listening with one ear as she was walking along the edge of the V-shaped pool with a trailing net to fish out the dead leaves. Her Chinese hat was mirrored in the pool in ripples of sun. Hands don't grow out of graves, she said, dumping another load of the soggy leaves into the wheelbarrow. You're full of slivovitz and salami, mama. This is the U.S.A.

Hold your tongue, said granny-anny in Croatian.

The land of the free, said Aunt V. You're hopeless, mama. Hands don't grow out of graves, not in this country. Don't you believe her, B.

I don't. Still the hand that won't stay buried is haunting me. I shut my eyes and there it is: my own hand like a naked tree shooting up out of the loose soil of my doll's grave.

A costumed doll of foreign descent. An alien like all my dolls. I have a collection. Each time Aunt V returns from a cruise with mom or a land-buying spree up and down the Costa del Sol, she brings home a doll. They're never babies, they are lady dolls with stupid wax faces and with their skirts and shawls glued together.

The last time she brought me a doll I cut off its head and tried to flush it down her toilet. But it kept bobbing up.

When little girls play with dolls, where is the father? Uncle D asked that night when we were having a grimy barbecue in the yard. He hadn't come to eat with us. He did not eat meat. He was nibbling on a raw mushroom as he sat in the cast iron chair away from the smoking barbecue pit under the purple sky. I was sitting at his feet in the gravel.

Do you like to play with dolls? he asked.

I'm too old, I said and rubbed my face to his knee.

Uncle D looked like a doll, short and neat in his safari coat as he emerged from the purple fog on the night pier a hundred years ago or more, it seems to me now. He was walking down the pier with short busy steps as if he were late for an important meeting though there was nothing in front of him at the end of the pier, only me and the rotting poles half submerged in the river. And behind him was W street, gray, with gray rows of trucks parked for the night as usual and the usual cops aiming their flashlights into the back of the trucks to catch the male lovers who might be hiding there. Some always were hiding in the back of the trucks, but they were three jumps ahead of the cops, they jumped down into the fog and vanished in a flutter of pigeon feathers.

The cops were blowing their whistles but Uncle D was not turning his head to look. He was walking in the opposite direction fast with his nose in the air and his hands in the pockets of his safari coat. He was dressed like a hunter. But he was a vegetarian. The hands of the clock in the Cutty Sark billboard above the old blind flop house were madly spinning. I stepped in his way and said hi.

He tried to ignore me, though maybe he didn't see me. Fat as I was, he may have thought I was nothing. His eyesight is poor and his glasses were fogged. It was night.

So he tried to step around me, but I wouldn't let him, I

grabbed him by his riding crop and assured him I wasn't a hooker. I was Aunt V's niece.

Of course! he said, removing his glasses and peering at me with eyes as small and cautious in the night as those of a mouse. Of course! His mustache was a charcoal smudge under his twitching nose and I thought how beautiful he was, like the tiny replica of a big game hunter. I'd seen him at Aunt V's before at various times, for though he was not one of her regular fellows—and in fact I've heard him say more than once that he was a lone wolf—he was, she'd say, her closest male companion and an investor, too, in real estate.

I don't think he remembered me from Adam or Eve, but at least he pretended, he said of course, of course, and then he inquired about Aunt V's health with such intense concern you'd believe she was sick in bed. Your dear dear aunt, how is she feeling?

But I played deaf to that question. Over on W street the parked trucks stood deserted and gigantic like sleeping elephants. The bearded poles in the water were swaying and creaking. Oh what a melancholy night, that night on the pier when I fell head first into love, down, down. I still am falling.

He flexed his arm and bent his head. The dial of his wrist watch sent out green signals. It's late, you ought to be in bed, he said. Come!

That was the moment when I decided to call him uncle. In his uplift shoes he was taller than I. Come! He had taken my arm. The Cutty Sark on the billboard was sailing the sky as he steered me past the trucks, the sleeping elephants, and to the house. There he waited by the stoop until I was safely through the door and had locked myself in.

The little girl is mother to her doll, he says, talking into the smoke as Aunt V throws hunks of beef on the smoking charcoal. She'll bathe and dress and comb her doll, she'll scold it and spank it and kiss it. But when she plays mother, where is the father? Absent most of the time or never invented.

I am crouching at his feet in the shadows. He fishes another raw mushroom out of the bowl and feeds it to me. It tastes of autumn leaves, the woods and Olli. I rub my cheek against the rough twill of his trousers.

Aunt V's head is a faceless copper pot above the fire. The sparks fly from her star-spangled blouse in the wind. She grabs the long two-pronged fork with her asbestos glove from Bloomingdales and turns the steaks, the bloody juice dripping and hissing. Delicious! A feast for the beast.

Too many little boys are ashamed to play mother, says Uncle D, turning his nose away from the smell of burned meat. The lion father, he says, will mother the cubs while the lioness is off, stalking her prey. The lioness is the hunter.

J won't touch her steak unless it's nearly raw. Oozing with blood. I've often asked myself why! Aunt V exclaims.

I feel Uncle D's shudder. Perhaps it is some form of atavism, he says in his blurred southern plantation voice. Uncle D has two different voices. Will J be joining us? he asks in his clipped city voice.

Who knows what J will do. Aunt V shakes her head. Run upstairs, will you, she says to me, slapping at a mosquito. See if your mother cares to join us. Run!

But I won't budge. His pants feel like a tree bark against my chin. I must run! he says, jumping up. He helps me on my feet with both his hands and kisses me below the hairline. Then he kisses Aunt V on both cheeks.

Dear V. Take care. Don't work too hard, he says. He is

patting her wrist in the firelight, his hand moving rapidly as if he were slapping her wrist.

His hands are baby soft and plump. But his torso is athletic. He works out regularly at the Y. I ask Aunt V if that's what he does for a living, but she says, no, he is a man of independent means. He is a gentleman and amateur scholar, clipping coupons, watching his weight, and doing research in she forgot what area.

The locker room area, says mom, biting off the tip of a fat black cigar. She has no more use for him than she has for the fellows, those who come in doubles and drink up the gin. Uncle D, of course, is an abstainer. But any of V's male callers, drunk or sober, fill mom with rage. If it's true, as V insists, that he prefers monkeys to people, why then doesn't he live in the zoo? mom demands. And why, she adds with a snarl, does he keep one hand in the pocket of his pants whenever he sits opposite V, munching health food and sipping peppermint tea?

I really wouldn't know, Aunt V says coyly. All I know is that he comes from an excellent background. His people struck it rich in the hotel business. They made a pile specializing in honeymooners. You might say he grew up to the tune of the Lohengrin march. No wonder he loathes Wagner. Every bed in their twelve bridal suites was shaped like a swan.

Where did you get that information! mom says fiercely.

Aunt V's painted eyelids are modestly lowered as she confides in a girlish whisper that she herself spent one of her honeymoons there with one of her X's. Jock or Jake: No matter which one of the two she was waiting for to stagger out of the stag bar and join her in the blooming garden of the booming hotel. She paced, feeling forsaken, when suddenly a dapper little man popped up from behind the azaleas, dressed in formal black and looking for all the world like the proverbial little man on her own unconsumed wedding cake. She waved at him. But he sped past her and up the terrace steps where his foot caught in the veil of a descending, aging bride. Poor D! She never would forget his mortified blush. But his mama was already there on the terrace and she had untangled him in no time.

She was a beautiful widow, Aunt V remembers, doe-eyed, Jewish or Egyptian and so poised, so sure of her place in the face of disaster or honeymooners. Elsa was her name and D adored her. It nearly killed him when she died. He'll never go to the altar.

I'm thankful for that, mom says flatly. If there's one thing I thank you for it's that you didn't try to drag me to the altar with that mother.

I too am thankful. He is a living doll and I wish he would elope with me to his retreat on Seesaw Island and love me to death in the Georgia moon in the azaleas. I'm thankful Aunt V crossed him off her list of potential husbands for mom or dads for me when she was frantically trying to make mom a legal wife at least on paper so I might be adopted without complications, though of course they hadn't even found me yet and maybe I was not yet born. But first things first. Aunt V had put it into her head that no adoption should be risked unless there was an upstanding male in the house. For mightn't they be investigated by some social worker who'd question them about their sex and snoop through their dirty linen?

There was no dirty linen, naturally. Flo changed the sheets every day. She polished the American eagle. Our house shone like a new silver dollar and only the alley and my mattress were reeking of piss. Flo said social workers didn't waste their time spying on rich people. They were paid to spy on the poor.

Mom, lolling in the love seat, infertile and languid, said, sure, and if worse came to worse they might always get a hold of a Brooks Brothers store window dummy and sit him up in the rocking chair on the stairs, on the second landing and point him out to the social worker: Pop's having his nap. He's been on his feet all day, minding the store.

A dummy might do for a husband, Aunt V agreed, recalling her married past. Still she would rather play it safe and find a more convincing head of the household, one of the fellows, for instance, provided he was in the clear with the police. She wouldn't want to see her name or mom's in the papers. As for the danger of blackmail, that she could handle, she supposed. She hadn't been through two husbands for nothing. What really worried her was J, what J might do. If the bridegroom was a sailor, her J-boy might fall for him hook, line and sinker and leave her poor roommate the fall guy. It had happened to other married couples.

No sailors. No stevedores or garbage collectors. Aunt V was casting for a normal introvert type with extrovert features and a good record with the army reserve or the secret service. She knew it was the type her J despised. Yet supposing they made such a lucky catch, mightn't she still run away with him simply because she despised him? She was so unpredictable, so impulsive, so very perverse. . . .Ah, if J only had faith! Then they could kneel together and pray to god to mail them the right husband and father material.

Empty beer cans rattle down the waterfront in the black wind. Mom's voice comes pushing through the night, up from the talking room through shattered mirrors: You bitch, you weren't content to saddle me with a brat, you had me down in your calendar as a June bride so you could have a ball and cry at the wedding . . .

Cars honk their horns. Rain hits the window panes like kernels of rice. A COLOR TV FREE FOR EVERY BOWERY BRIDE, says my transistor. YOUR HONEYMOON CAN BE YOUR MONEYMOON. DEPOSIT BEFORE YOU EARN.

You bitch, I hear mom say. You had it figured to a T-bone, a church wedding, holy JC, then off for the country and an unholy bash with the girls in Sappho's Silo. You were still shopping for a husband for me when you had already set the date for my wedding. Man you were itching to see me dressed up as bride for a day in 69 yards of ruffles and grandpa's longjohns under the petticoat. Man, you were wetting your drawers to watch me prance up the aisle and say I do to some cocksucking mother. Only you couldn't dig up the right sucker. None wanted to be groom, each had his heart set on being the bride, each wanted to wear the veil and the orange blossoms and toss the bouquet to his fellow mother.

The rain is coming down in buckets. Aunt V is in tears. J, lover, don't be mean to me, don't curse your poor V wife, she's too romantic and doesn't she know it, so feminine it hurts her you do know where, she can't help crying, don't blame her for what she can't help, she cries at every wedding and funeral . . .

Over my dead body you'll cry at *my* funeral! No stinking undertaker is going to shoot *me* up with embalming fluid.

I'm leaving my ravaged body to science. Get me a pencil, I'll put it in writing, I'll write it right here on the wall.

Hush love, you couldn't write your name, you're so inebriated. . . .

Inebriated, hoho, three sheets in the wind, but not a living thing in the oven. . . OK. . . I'll sign *your* name, sister. I'll will them *your* ravaged body. They already have your tubes . . . How much does a stiff bring these days? Call up the city morgue and ask for the price list . . .

Nine point nine of the national gross, my transistor says under the pillow. THE BABY BUST IS ON & THOUGH BIRTH STILL OUTNUMBERS DEATH TWO TO ONE THE TEENAGE INDUSTRY IS SERIOUSLY CONSIDERING A SWITCH TO SENIOR CITIZEN NECESSITIES. . . .

The announcer's crackling voice fades into silence. Somewhere far away in the wet night a baby is crying. But from the talking room downstairs not a word, not a snivel or snicker. Have they dropped dead? The wind makes a sharp turn and suddenly I hear mom's voice again, only this time it is a desperate cry: Hold me, V, hold me or I shall die. . . . Don't let me die, V, hold me. . . .

The pornography of death, Uncle D said to no one as he came striding down the pier in the sunset; blinking and cracking his riding crop at no one or at old Miss Liberty who stood with her torch at the bleeding mouth of the harbor, dowdy, mildewy and overweight like me far out in the smog.

Again I thought it odd that he carried that riding crop when he had so much respect for animals he wouldn't even mount a horse, let alone whip one, as he had explained to me. The little whip, he had explained, was simply a device to make him feel safer along the waterfront or in the park of this deadly city. But mom had said in the talking room to Aunt V that she bet her bottom dollar he had a whole collection of riding crops as well as bullwhips, handcuffs, brass knuckles, bicycle chains and maybe a big empty cage for him to sit in or have somebody else locked up in. Why else should his apartment be off-limits for V, his bosom friend and closest financial advisor? Why didn't he invite her for tea the way she invited him? Didn't he know that she was passing by his co-op highrise all the time on her way to her damned therapist, masseuse or dentist? The three were plying their dubious trades in the same building with a view to the park, a block or so from where he was plying his dubious trade behind drawn shades, mom had said. Something fishy here, she said, I smell a rat.

A water rat. Each time he finds me waiting for him at the end of the pier he jumps and consults his wristwatch. I must go! I'm late! he cries though he never says where he must go or why he is late. Never. He fidgets with his riding crop and kicks an empty whisky bottle into the sunset. But finally he resigns himself to me and sits down by my side on one of the rotting poles. The Jersey coast flares up like a burning dream. A flat black coal barge on the river is making waves and now the poles underneath us begin to groan. They sway and shiver. I shiver with love but he blames the stiff breeze, and he removes his safari coat to put over my trembling shoulders.

Why do I pick that moment to ask him about his collection of bullwhips and cages?

Bullwhips and cages! He stares at me with incredulous

eyes. He takes off his glasses and wipes them. Where on earth did you hear that story!

I hug myself under his coat and say that I have heard it through a wall, though maybe I only dreamed it.

You dreamed it? He looks at me closely. Without the glasses his mouse eyes are sad. Ah, children are dangerous eavesdroppers, and in their dreams they eavesdrop on themselves, he says. I speak from experience. I eavesdropped in my sleep as a small boy. We lived on the ground floor of our hotel and not a night went by that I didn't listen in on the ocean waves and the honeymooners. Not a sound escaped me. I heard every wave, every whisper.

Uncle D bends his face toward me. YOU DO / I DON'T / NOT NOW / FOR NEVERMORE / TILL DEATH, he remembers, rubbing the tip of his nose in his palm. He says he tried to make the words into a poem, but nothing much came of it. He says he eavesdropped on love before he had learned to tell a man from a woman. He still does find it difficult to tell, which, however, is not surprising, considering the present unisex trend.

It's not my cup of tea, says Uncle D. I yearn for the good old days.

His eyes are moist. But that is because of the wind. He sits in his bush shirt. He sneezes. I'm afraid he might want his coat back, but he doesn't ask me for it, he says he is warming himself by the gaslight of those days forever gone when a man did not have to look at a woman to know that she was a woman, when he could tell her sex at once by the subtle music of her garments—the rustle of the bustle, the froufrou of the frillies, the swish of the trailing train. It was a musical world of innuendos and Bishop sleeves. No lady worthy of that name would have dared expose here bare arms in the street.

I hide my bare fat arms under his coat. Our lives, Uncle D says, blinking against the wind, have become too garish, too barefaced. He longs for the mauve era when a lady's face was swathed in veils and shaded by a parasol at Biarritz; when she would sit immobilized at the Ritz in her stiff corset, the way his mother's mother had sat for her honeymoon picture, immobilized by whalebone stays in the Prater.

Ah, for the hourglass waist! The tied ankles! The thrust of the bust! he exclaims, throwing his chest out. Ah, for the S-shaped silhouette which transformed the female form into a galleon figure nailed fast to the ship's prow! But all this is done with—fini, says Uncle D, wiping his eyes. Wiped out, he says, shading his eyes, by the suffragettes and Isadora Duncan.

He looks depressed, but all at once he has leaped up, elated, and for a moment he stands over me and so close to me I can hear his heart beat. But it is my own heart I hear under the safari coat. Excuse me, please, he says, and my body goes limp as his hand feels down the inside pocket of that coat and comes out with a pair of binoculars.

Excuse me, he says again, stepping away from me and to the very edge of the pier. There he trains the binoculars on a passing ship—to spy the galleon figure at the prow? But the ship is a Russian freighter. I can see it with the naked eye — the big red star, and on the deck the sailors stripped to the waist. Two sailors are wrestling. The others watch. Uncle D watches until the freighter is a mere toy in the mist.

The *Alexander Pushkin,* he says, glancing first at the clock in the Cutty Sark billboard, and then at his wristwatch. Good heavens! I'm late! I must run!

Run, run as fast as you can, run, Uncle D, forget that I am still wearing your coat so I can take it home and hide it under my mattress and use it for my pillow every night.

But Uncle D never forgets. Already he has snatched the coat off my shoulders. He plants a make-believe kiss atop my head, and then he is off, not even cracking his whip.

A tiny, pallid sickle of a moon hangs upside down from Miss Liberty's torch. If I wore a corset and tied my ankles, could I make him fall in love with me? Is he or is he not in love with Aunt V? Mom thinks he is. But she suspects every man.

I feel the bearded pole rock under me. The waves lap gently, washing beer cans, condoms and candy wrappers ashore and back out to sea.

She isn't home when I let myself in. She must be combing the bars for mom who has disappeared again, though Flo says, how could she when she never was here anyhow?

Flo is upstairs in their bedroom, changing the purple sheets. I wander into their bathroom which is the grandest in the house. Mine is full of floating toy boats, but theirs has a sunken tub with a rubber mermaid from Coney Island and a Nepal flag half-staff above the tub, and goat skins from the Greek islands all over the floor, and a Spanish crucifix by the marble sink which is smooth and round and pink like my belly. The toothpaste is pink. I like to watch mom brush her teeth with a brush so worn down it hasn't a bristle left. (Aunt V bought her an electric toothbrush at Bloomingdales, but mom must have either lost it or thrown it away.) I like her candy smell of peppermint toothpaste and gin. I like to hear her tell Aunt V through the pink toothpaste foam: You go to hell.

To hell, mom said, with your dreams about a lost key to the right door or a found key to the wrong door, to hell with your clocks and cocks and tongues and mermaids in aspic.

Consult your dream book. You're not on my couch. Your night life bores me to death.

Mom was at her best in the morning when she had a big head which made her act meaner than ever toward Aunt V. But to me she was sweet, she gave me a sweet toothpaste kiss and said, for chrissake get that woman out of here before I kill her, take her to a museum, anything, just get her off my back. I'll pay you for it.

But usually Aunt V was busy at her plush real estate office, buying, selling, and conniving over the phone while mom would be sleeping late into the day and sometimes into the night. The noon sun was trying to break through the heavy curtains as I crept into the bedroom where mom was snoring her life away under the covers. Even her head was under cover, and if it hadn't been for her noisy snoring, she might have been a dummy under the blankets and sheets. I rattled the aspirin bottle above the pillow but she slept like a bear and nothing would wake her up, not even the water as I made for the bathroom and turned the faucets on full blast to take a bubble bath with the rubber mermaid.

Niagara Falls. But mom slept. I emptied the whole bottle of Aunt V's BONNE NUIT CHERIE into the tub. Her precious perfume, one million bucks an ounce, stank until the bubbles vanished. I gagged and took a hot shower. All the mirrors were steamed over, the fogs swirled and descended, but mom was snoring, I squeezed out mom's pink toothpaste and ate some, I squeezed out a B on my tongue, and then another B on the mirror, and still another until the mirror was covered with B's.

Flo has stripped the king sized beauty rest mattress of last night's sheet. The ticking, blue and white summer stripes, makes me think of the big striped umbrella on granny-anny's lawn. The garden umbrella broke during Hurricane Lizzy but granny-anny was already dead or so they pretend.

Flo opens a window and flaps out the fresh sheet. There is a sea wind and the sheet snaps out like a purple sail. It makes me homesick for mom and I ask Flo, where is she? Where's my dad, Flo asks back. If you find him for me I'll find your mom for you. So we toss the ball back and forth and sometimes we change places and I ask her to find me a dad. It is an old game between us. We play it now as I help her make up the bed. She has taught me how to fold the bottom sheet neat at the corners the way they do it in the hospitals. A hundred years ago or more Flo tried to be a nurse. But all they let her do in the all white cancer ward for half dead whites was to empty the bedpans.

Whenever mom was gone from the house which was always, Aunt V would check the hospital wards and the city morgue, though first of all she would check BANGS of course. I myself once tried to look for mom there, but the bouncer wouldn't let me through the door, though the door was open long enough for me to spy mom's face liquid in the steamed mirror behind the bar.

B for BULIMIA, BANGS, or BOMBS. A firecracker explodes in the night, or is it a cherry bomb, though it is not the 4th of J else we would be in granny-anny's hills, with me and Olli balling in the weeds behind the garbage dump under a cluster of stars dripping honey.

A fire engine shrieks through the rain. It comes to a

sudden halt and I wonder did a real bomb explode on the pier and blow it up, all the way up to the moon? The moon is littered with bits of rotted wood and chunks of cement. What place is there left for me to meet Uncle D in the sunset?

We met at BANGS, but that was years ago and by sheer accident, Aunt V says to mom into the roaring night. Since then much water has passed under Queensborough Bridge, and how often haven't you promised me since that never would you set foot into that vile bar again?

No answer from mom.

Aunt V coughs noisily—to wake her up? For mom might well be asleep. Aunt V claps her hands and says, you've broken your promise time and again—how many times have you lied?

No answer from mom.

A teakettle whistles. Aunt V must be brewing herself a pot of strong tea. For she is weary to the bone, having searched for mom in every low bar, though none, she says, is quite as low as BANGS which is the lower depth. You can't sink lower.

Funnybone china clatter of cup against saucer. Tuning fork ping of teaspoon and sugar tongs. Aunt V plays hostess to herself. She pours. How many lumps? No lemon, honey. Maybe a drop of rum.

You keep asking, she says (though mom has asked nothing of course) why I ventured into BANGS at all that wet afternoon of our fatal encounter. Frankly I don't remember. I may have wanted to get out of the rain. Naturally I had *heard* of BANGS as who hasn't? It's been raided often enough. No, love, I wouldn't say I expected a classy joint like the Plaza but I certainly wasn't prepared for a whorehouse either, I mean the absolute vulgarity of the place, black tablecloths full of cigarette burns, moth-chewed velvet drapes and filthy carpets and plaster statues of naked nymphos inscribed with such obscene graffitti even you, J, would blush if you bothered to read them though of course the place is so poorly lighted you can't even read the menu. I dare say, B—I take it she is Mrs. Bangs—doesn't enrich Con Ed.

Another teeny weeny drop of rum, sweetie? Say when. WHEN!

Wow! Musta spilled half a pint into the low, low décolleté of my tea rose frou-frou taffeta tea gown from Dallas Texas.

Dear me. What a mess, says Aunt V, drying herself with wads of pink toilet paper. No, no, a hundred times no, J, BANGS never could be my cup of tea, the fems there are either terribly low class or chronically nympho—present company excluded, J— and as for the middle-aged johns at the bar the less said the better, they pay through the nose for watered-down booze to watch you and your likes carry on, jesus, I know those commuting family men, I've sold them property in Chappaqua, they masturbate under the car coat, and then they drive off to the Union Club to tell the boys how we women abuse our right to vote.

Aunt V takes a deep breath and kicks the wad of toilet paper into the fire. No, J, you wouldn't get your jollies from them, no, it's the repulsive waitresses you are after, the table-hopping hepped-up broads in their jump suits, dear christ, figures like jellyfish, the fattest one, the one with acne, how she pushed her behind against you when she stomped into the girls room like a stormtrooper out for blood. But let some guy complain of the cockroach in his

manhattan and she screams him down like the whore she is:
DUMKOPF! WHY DIDNTYA SAY YA WANTED A
CHERRY! I almost threw up. And the smell! A decent
fellow wouldn't touch that creature if you paid him for it.
But you, J, you touched her, and don't you dare lie to me! I
saw you! I saw you make it with her in the girls room.

Aunt V must have jumped up from the oriental divan
and sent the cushions flying and the tea wagon spinning
into eternity. She moans oh why won't mom be happy
unless she wallows in depravity? Surely it was god's will that
brought them together that faraway afternoon at BANGS
in the rain. Then mom was the desperate one. She cried on
her shoulder then, Aunt V remembers with a moan as sad as
the wind.

My J, my terrible angel, why are you set on destroying us
both?

No answer from mom. Perhaps she is asleep on the floor,
on the bear rug. Perhaps she is not in the house at all.

Mom's bleach blond head growing out dark at the roots at
BANGS in the twilight. Mom's shaggy head crying on Aunt
V's shoulder, begging to be saved—from what? Mom had
been drifting endlessly, Aunt V might say, drifting in and
out through many ports, through many murky backwaters
with the scum, and there was nothing she hadn't tried to
prevent her from going under, nothing, that is, except to
find honest work. Perhaps that solution never had entered
her head, though everything else had entered it, and she
had drifted through all the ups and all the downs and all the
outs, only to drift back in the end to the old bottle.

Can you spare a butt, sister? mom had asked her that late,
memory-blurred afternoon when the rains had been whip-

ping the 9th precinct and an old drunk had drifted into BANGS dripping wet to cry that the world was scheduled to blow itself up in less than a minute.

Repent, sisters.

Aunt V was sitting at the far end of the bar, consoling a fugitive housewife from Ozone Park, and she was unaware of mom until the drunk made his doleful entrance. Then she looked behind her and there stood mom. The drunk had already been bounced, but mom was still standing behind her, disheveled, underfed, with one front tooth missing and reminding her, Aunt V might reminisce, of a juvenile delinquent in his big brother's sweat shirt and dungarees.

Ragged fingernails. A hacking cough. Sallow skin. But oh, the Grecian mouth was that of a god, with the lower lip slowly curling inside out like a secret second tongue while the huge amber eyes were swimming among the bottles in the amber mirror of BANGS' long bar.

Aunt V slipped the housewife from Ozone Park a few bucks and with a chaste kiss on the cheek advised her to take a cab back to her husband and children.

A Spanish guitar was twanging in the long rain.

Sister, can you spare a cig?

Here, take all of them. Take them, please. I'm trying to quit.

Mom took them, cigarette case and all. A silver case engraved with love from J for Jake or Jock. Mom didn't wait to read the inscription, she stuffed it down her dungarees where it fell through a hole in the pocket and into the spittoon under the bar.

But neither of them noticed the loss, mom was too drunk and Aunt V was already too bewitched to notice anything except those eyes, that mouth, she might recall as she would search the hall mirror for a reflection of their lost afternoon when mom's drooping head had slowly come to rest on Aunt V's shoulder.

Another drink, girls?

Eyelashes send butterfly kisses. Fingertips stroke palm. Fortune teller V's hand is blessed with the clairvoyant eye—second sight handed down to her by gypsy ancestors who traveled steep sleep roads in the rain of Croatian mountains, with their bears on chains, dripping wet.

Mom's hand, ragged nails hidden, is lying palm up in a puddle of spilled gin. Fantastic life line! Talent for discipline. A stranger has just stepped into your life and I see a great deal of money coming your way. Also a pleasure cruise through the Aegean. Artistic endeavors, I can't be quite sure in what area. But I can sense it. . . . Creative talent is written all over you. All over. . . .

Girls, please! Not at the *bar*!

How many parting shots for mom, each shot of gin the last, the one for the road? It must have been dark when she had finally sleepwalked out into the downpour, with Aunt V as her seeing eye. The street had been deserted. There had been no one, only a hot dog vendor like an enraged puppet by his overturned stand in the flood, and V&J wrapped in one plastic sheet, in silence.

There had been no one else for them in all the world, not even me, I wasn't even an idea then, as their union, Aunt V might say, was blessed enough. They were wrapped up in themselves, their love, their mutual trust, and returning from work, Aunt V could be sure to find mom at home, resting up after those years of drifting through treacherous waters. She might sleep in the sun on the roof or read a comic book or Great Expectations. It was the only novel she had read and she knew it by heart, often reading through her sleep, her dreams. Then she might cry, hold me, hold me, Miss Havisham! It might wake Aunt V briefly, but never make her jealous. She was that sure of mom's absolute loyalty.

They always went to bed at the same hour. Sometimes mom never got out of bed. She was resting, she was losing that starved look, though she didn't eat as properly as she should have, she ate mostly potato chips. They were spilled all over the sheets and the floors and the chairs and the stairs. Wherever they walked, sat or lay there was that autumn rustle of fallen leaves, and tonight I too hear the fallen leaves in my own bed. Mom's nether world shadows in the hollows of her cheeks and under her eyes had not disappeared, but they showed less because she was now deeply tanned—her golden angel! Aunt V marveled into the mirror.

Yes, the good life was bringing out the best points in her boy, she marveled, comparing figures as they swayed nude in the triple mirror: 3 J's, 3 V's under a baldachin borne by a fat cherub. My angel, she whispered. And she slipped the ring with the milky opal off her little finger and pressed it like a seal between her angel's thighs.

3 V's on their knees. 3 J's erect like three slim columns — thighs locked, lips opened wide. 3 milky opals peering through brown seaweeds.

With this ring, Aunt V intones. And she slips it on mom's little finger under the ceremonial baldachin.

When was it that mom stopped wearing the opal, explaining, when Aunt V asked why, that it made her look too much like a faggot? Aunt V couldn't quite remember the day. But she all too clearly remembered the night when she saw the sacred ring dangling from a black shoe lace down the repulsive bosom of that fat waitress at BANGS. Aunt V made a grab for it. She tore the shoe lace, snatched the ring and fled as fast as she could in her tight cowboy boots, pursued by the screaming waitress who threatened to kill her. (She would have killed you. She is a karate expert, mom will say coldly whenever the mystery of the ring is revived.)

Thank god Aunt V had been able to escape with her life—into the church of St. V, she remembered, crossing herself. There she had knelt by the altar in prayer for J and laid the ring as an offering at the gilded feet of Santa Veronica, Aunt V's own patroness and loyal guardian.

The ring has caused their first grim fight. Mom of course pleads innocent, swearing she must have dropped it some place on her way to the liquor store. Cross my heart and hope to die. She swears she hasn't the faintest idea what the screaming is all about, the waitress whoever she is or isn't must have found the ring in the street. Finders keepers.

Losers weepers. Aunt V swallows hard. She swallows her tears and dares mom to accompany her to BANGS this minute and repeat her story word for word in front of the fat homewrecking waitress whore.

But mom says in a stony voice that she is through with BANGS. Not ten horses could drag her there again. And how is it, she asks, that V has been there again? What was V after?

You! screams Aunt V. I was going after *you*! I didn't find you home when I got back from work bone tired. How can an angel be so cruel? I sat by the phone till all hours, waiting to hear from you. You might have had an accident. Your perfect body! I saw your body lying mutilated and unclaimed at the morgue.

BANGS is no morgue, the angel says coldly. The only morgue I've ever lain in is your godawful house.

Aunt V's cozy nest a morgue! And this on their first anniversary when they had planned to celebrate. But naturally J forgot. She forgot that V has reserved a table for two in the private dining room of LA POULE ENCHAINEE.

Of course her J has no sense of time. She has been drifting far too long in the rain to remember what date she forgot to keep or where she lost what.

I do understand your problem—up to a point, says Aunt V, and I am ready to forgive and forget the whole episode, including the ring. It may still turn out for the best. Unless it's your birthstone, the opal is said to bring bad luck. Bad luck: the fact hit me between the eyes in St. V's empty church where I left it on the altar. I wonder if somebody found it—a nun perhaps?

Finders sleepers. They'll never guess that I found the ring, though not on any altar. I found it in a trash can in the street and it is tiny, the opal is no bigger than an apple seed. Yet what fire! I lick it till it shines and watch the tiny flames wriggle and leap. I've decided to make it my birthstone which is easy since any day of the year might by my birthday and any stone on earth my lucky stone.

Once, not too long ago on the pier while the sun was rapidly drowning, I offered the ring to Uncle D if he promised to wear it on a chain under his bush shirt. But he said he was already wearing a holy medal, St. Francis on a thin silver chain. Uncle D said he wasn't a catholic, he was a freethinker, though closely tied in spirit to St. Francis because of that mild brother's love for birds and beasts.

You keep your ring, said Uncle D, my birthstone is not the opal, it is the carbuncle, but thank you anyway, what time is it, dear me! I must run!

Run sheep run, Aunt V says it would be a blessing from heaven if mom consulted a watch, not constantly like Uncle D, but at least once in a while. But that, she admits, is a pipe dream, and the shock proof waterproof skin diver watch she bought for an anniversary present and strapped around mom's wrist so tight it turned the skin blue got lost again the next day, maybe to the same hideous waitress. Enough. Her analyst has advised her to cool it and send mom up to the office for therapy.

Nobody's going to fuck my head, mom said when Aunt V relayed the good doctor's message.

No therapy. Aunt V crosses it off the list. He has encouraged her to make up a list of workable ideas for J-keeping. The list includes me. Am I her analyst's idea? Is doc my dad? But I am still at the very bottom of the list, for surely there must be other occupations than motherhood to keep her boy at home, says Aunt V, chewing the pencil stub.

Housework is out, of course. Mom wouldn't think of it, or if she did, Flo would quit. She almost quit that time mom staggered into the kitchen by mistake, demanding where the hell was she, was she on the shuttle train?

Make her stop drinking? But mom won't stop unless she can be steered into a structured existence, or so the shrink seems to think, and really Aunt V is not surprised when her angel complains that she is bored to extinction. For how can she fail to be bored since she does absolutely nothing except sleep, drink and read about supermouse and a dead spinster in an old wedding gown! No adult can afford to be that lazy, though at least her J hasn't strayed again, not since that fated night, not to her knowledge, Aunt V might think, sniffing mom's hair for a strange scent, holding mom's T-shirt under the lamp to examine it for lipstick stains, a stranger's lipstick. No guilty evidence as yet. So far so good. But how long will the armistice last? How long before Aunt V will have to face another night of torture and deadly visions alone by the phone?

Back to the list. An outside job for J? A job outside of the house, that is. But that would defeat the chief purpose which is to keep her inside the house. Tear up the list. Start a fresh legal pad. Concentrate, old girl. Aunt V takes a deep breath. She picks up an ink pen and writes

CREATIVENESS

in purple letters diagonally across the yellow page. At that moment all the lights in the house go out. I've blown a fuse! mom cries from the black talking room.

But Aunt V isn't put out by the dark. She has seen the light. (And didn't she feel her angel's creative potential already at BANGS?) There's nothing quite like creativity to keep a body occupied at home and out of mischief. It's fun to create, it's healthy, everybody does it, god does it, it's patriotic, and where was it that she read about the habitual jail breaker who turned so gentle after they let him play with a box of paints, so grateful to be in jail, he begged them to keep him for life. They might have kept him. But a guard shot him dead by mistake, assuming he was about to break out again when he was merely jogging for his health.

That's life for you. But nobody is going to shoot her J-bird. She will be safe at home, a real home body at long last. Aunt V looks transfigured as she smiles down upon the word CREATIVENESS which has begun to glow in the dark with its own magic.

Stop eating! Aunt V said to me. Stop hollering for extras, cut out the chocolate fudge sundaes and do something creative instead, learn to play the guitar, or write your memoirs, OK, you paint, you may borrow my paints, just make sure you use them creatively. When I return with your mom from our Aegean cruise I expect to find you umpty pounds lighter, rid of all the humpty dumpty surplus fat.

Create, lose weight. I squirted her oil paints all over their triple mirrors and bedroom walls. The paints were beautiful. I sang out their names. I loved the sound of ultramarine and I sang it for hours to the tune of Anchors Away.

Anchors Away! I drowned their mattress in waves of ultramarine. I sang, I bounced on the waves.

Was I still on the list that night when the house blacked out and Aunt V went to the talking room to light the candles in the Spanish candelabra? J's head swam in the candle light in the V lap. Aunt V was stroking mom's hair, ruffling and smoothing it, as she spoke, tentatively at first, of the joy of creating things, and how she might be mentally unbalanced today had not her analyst, or one of them, suggested that she fill her spare time sketching and painting.

It saved my sanity, she says. And then as if the thought has hit her only now, she adds in the lightest possible tone: Speaking of spare time (and you have plenty of that!) why don't *you* get into something creative?

Scratch the top of my head, says mom. Harder! Beautiful. Keep scratching.

Aunt V's crimson fingernails are raking through mom's streaked weedy hair. Mom shuts her eyes and purrs, while Aunt V, always keeping up that same light tone, says: Why don't *you* get into something like painting. It's such great fun. No sweat. And so gratifying for the ego.

Keep scratching! Harder! mom commands.

Obediently Aunt V continues to scratch. There's that spare room upstairs which no one is using, it's full of books, full of rubbish, and they might clean it out and make it over into a studio, she says, unaware of course that it's my future nursery she's contemplating. They might paint it white and put in big mirrors so mom can paint herself from life, she says, but all at once stops short and bites her lips. For what if mom says yes and then insists on hiring male and female models, for study purposes, supposedly?

For a dreadful second an orgy of naked bodies, with mom's in the center, flashes through Aunt V's mind and she cries out as though in agonies of pain: No! Never! No!

What the hell's the matter with you? mom demands, opening her eyes.

And Aunt V, still shaken by the imagined orgy in that spare room (my room! but she doesn't know!) abandons all diplomacy and shoots mom's question back at her (what the hell's the matter with *you*, J, if one may be permitted to ask!) and then, expecting no reply of course, she proceeds to accuse mom of laziness and selfishness and drunkenness and a whole lot of other vices in one furious rush. Mom's drinking will be the death of their marriage and unless she submits to some kind of daily routine (obviously painting is out, Aunt V remarks as an aside, relieved at least for a second, that she hears no objection from mom) unless mom keeps herself busy with some sort of creative activity like music, poetry or needlework, she'll end up in the gutter for sure.

Needlework! Mom bursts into laughter, her head bobs up and down in the V lap. What sort of needle do you have in mind, doll?

I have work in mind, Aunt V says grimly, for the vision of that orgy is flashing up again pink and evil. She's gotten to her feet, having first moved mom's head onto a pillow quite gently, really, considering that evil vision. The candles shake in the candelabra as she begins to pace with heavy steps, restlessly, in desperation the way she will pace the hospital corridors months later, waiting for mom to give birth to me or my twin.

Work. But what kind? she wonders, pacing in the candlelight, removing the remains of a horsefly which has expired on the keyboard of the antique spinet. Aunt V says that she taught herself to play the piano for she loves music, BONNE NUIT CHERIE or the moonlight sonata, and she still practices whenever her crowded schedule lets her, she says, squinting down at the keyboard and running her thumb over it in a pretty glissando. Perhaps mom should learn to play the piano. It would give her something to do. Four hours of practice each day: that should teach her discipline, says Aunt V.

Discipline! Mom smacks her thigh with her flat hand and laughs out loud.

Yes, discipline! Aunt V cries, slamming the spinet lid shut. Life isn't a mindless orgy of drunken free-for-all romps, life requires sacrifices you don't want to make, you'll have to make them, do it for me, you are so gifted, I felt the poetry in you at BANGS...

(My god, I'm softening again, Aunt V thinks, feeling suddenly weak in the groin.)

Poetry, my angel, yes, she continues with a catch in her throat, a poem a day...It's a small enough favor to ask in return for all I've done for you, do it for me, say yes, do, do....

O blessed night. Aunt V has snuffed out the candles, and now she kneels and buries her head between mom's knees, do it, but suddenly the crystal chandelier glares down on them ice cold and fiercely bright from the talking room ceiling. The lights are back on all over the house. The house is lit from top to bottom, the TV and the radios are shrieking. A police siren shrieks murder and mom jumps up and proceeds to get terribly drunk and soon she is shouting terrible things through the window, down into the deserted alley.

It was an ominous start, that night before her angel was supposed to turn over a new leaf, Aunt V might sigh. There had been much bitterness, much broken glass. Still she had kept her faith and bought a beautiful notebook for mom to write down her thoughts, a looseleaf notebook bound in genuine calf imported from Italy. Whatever expensive gift Aunt V would buy her, mom was sure to lose the following day. But she did not lose that notebook. It still exists. I've seen it on Aunt V's vanity table. I've opened it more than once to the first page, the one single line there in mom's ink-loaded hand which is as awkward as my own hand. JEDER ENGEL IST SCHRECKLICH.

I don't think she knows the language. I think she must have copied the words letter for letter from one of those German booklets Q might strew about granny-anny's place in the hills where she and the other sisters, too many of them, would spend the weekend. Q knows the language, she was a WAC stationed in Heidelberg which she says is one heap of ruins, the whole castle bombed out, she says, centuries before the bomb was invented.

Yes, mom must have copied the line from Q's book and I've often seen the two together under the plum tree, mom making believe she was reading over Q's bare, snow white shoulder as Q, her red hair streaming into her eyes, would sit in silence, with a small book in her lap.

JEDER ENGEL IST SCHRECKLICH. I copied it from mom's notebook and took it to the pier in the wind for Uncle D to translate. But he said it was impossible. The SCHRECK was untranslatable, he said. EVERY ANGEL IS: He was willing to commit himself that far but no further.

Every angel . . . There's nothing else inside that book, not another line or word. The pages are empty. But on the page next to the last, in the left corner, I've noticed a small cross in ink. I doubt that anyone outside of me has noticed it. Mom's unwritten poems are lying on the vanity table and sometimes Aunt V will open the book and stare at the single line and speak the first letter. J.

SCHRECKS READYMADE PICKMEUP CAKEMIX FOR PROCESSED ANGELS. But the transistor under my pillow is dead and I must have tuned in on a dream or hit a quiet spot in Alaska. Switch stations. FOUL RAINS FOR THE REST OF THE NIGHT. FLY V&J AND LOSE YOUR LUGGAGE. YOU ARE LISTENING TO YOUR FAVORITE WEATHERMAN.

Get out of my hair, mom says, shaking the rain out of her hair in the talking room below though her voice sounds more distant, as if it came out of the boarded-up house next door, the condemned house Aunt V bought as a safe investment although it isn't safe to be lived in of course. You can hear it fall apart—loose boards rattle and crack, window panes crack and break as the rain drips steadily through the leaks in the roof. And all these sounds beat against mom's voice: Get out of my hair.

Or is it Aunt V I hear? But maybe they are saying it together and maybe it's me they want out of their hair, first they wished me in and now they want me out, the brat, the bat, I'm their idea, swoosh! I swish back and forth between them. Shall I fly into mom's mouth? If she swallows me I'll be safe and warm inside her dark belly.

I'm patting my own big belly and feel the flutter of a bird or bat. The brat, mom says of me to hurt Aunt V. But when mom and I are alone together which happens rarely she calls me kid, OK kid, you do what you like, kid, whatever you say kid, I have a terrible head.

She had a terrible head that time she hurt me, by accident, to be sure, for never would she hurt me on purpose, never. But she was badly hung over, or hung, she might say. I'm hung, kid leave me alone.

She was soaking in the hot tub with the rubbermermaid from Coney Island and a cold washcloth green over her face. I still was little then, but I was already fat and when I sneaked into the tub with her I caused a flood. The water spilled over the goatskin rugs and washed the mermaid ashore. Mom's head went under. I pulled it back by the hair and saved her from drowning. But I had scared her half to death. She yelled at me. She chased me out of the tub and hurled a cake of soap at me so hard it gave me a large bump under one eye.

A yellow cake of almond soap shaped like an egg: I picked it up from the floor to take with me. Mom's face had disappeared again under the green washcloth. I bawled and shuffled off to my room, leaving a long, wet track between us. The bump showed in the mirror purple and blue. I bawled and wished for the bump to stay for ever. I knocked on wood.

My poor, poor baby! cried Aunt V when she came home after dark. What happened to your face! she cried, dropping her attaché case. Who hit you, baby?

Nobody, I said. I didn't look at mom nor did she look at me, she pretended to watch TV, a frontier fistfight. Aunt V wailed: Who hit my baby! I said I slipped on my bathroom floor and fell against my new submarine which was a recent gift from Aunt V. It almost knocked my eye out, I said.

Oh the poor baby! Aunt V bent down to examine the bump and kiss it away. But I kicked her.

I must say! she cried, turning to mom. You might have kept an eye on your daughter! Those toys of hers all over the floor—battleships and submarines and destroyers. The child might have killed herself. But I suppose you weren't at home when she fell. You never are at home.

Mom looked up from a dead body under a cactus tree on TV. She looked straight at me and said, I'm sorry I hit you, kid.

You didn't! Aunt V gasped. How could you hit an innocent child! What did she do!

Nothing, mom said. We were looking at each other. I'm sorry it happened, kid, she said. She was still speaking to me alone, though her eyes were meeting Aunt V's in the mirror. She said, I don't know what got into me. I had a terrible head.

I squeezed the bruise in the mirror. I said I hurt, but mom could not hear me. She had turned up the TV. They were shooting it out in the desert. Aunt V switched it off. Of course you had a head, she said, who wouldn't after a night of poker and enough boilermakers to blast a battleship.

I'm hurting, I moaned into the mirror.

The next time you feel like hitting somebody, hit me! I'm used to it, Aunt V said in a wounded tone. She pulled the leather skirt up over her thigh to show the bruises.

I said I was sorry, said mom. What do you want me to do — go down on my knees?

She looked disheveled and guilty like that stray sheep dog who'd come to granny-anny's kitchen door each time it rained. Mom was like that dog. I loved her. I was sorry for nothing. Aunt V was fingering the welt at the back of her thigh, complaining how she hurt so much she had barely been able to sit down at the office.

I'm sorry, mom growled. She wagged her head and put her grimy paws on Aunt V's shoulders. Her eyes were black behind the shaggy hair. The mirror was dark and wet.

I went upstairs. I locked myself in and washed with mom's almond soap.

Mom out of the rain and back in the fold—chastened, Aunt V believes each time mom has returned from another spree at the eleventh hour, just as Aunt V might be about to give her up. And though mom has been found again Aunt V might yet continue to search for her out of sheer habit.

She might be at the other end of town, searching, as mom would crawl out of a cab and up our stoop, though sometimes she might mistake the condemned house for our house and ask the driver to stop where nobody lives. Then she would knock at the boarded-up door in the black of night and hit the boards with both fists—Open up! Let me in!—while Aunt V would be combing BANGS and the other bars and maybe the city morgue.

72

Let me out! mom would cry, hammering against the boards, imagining that someone had locked her up inside the dead house.

I lock my door every night although Aunt V has forbidden it time and again. For there's danger, she says, in too much safety as my lock might get jammed and I won't be able to escape in case there should be a fire or a child molester climbing through the window. Hand me that key, child! she'd command, forgetting how many keys I've handed her. It never has occurred to her that she might have the lock removed, for she doesn't know how easy it is for me to find another key. She doesn't know how I fish them out of the river with a magnet tied to a long fishing line. The bottom of the river is thick with keys that people have lost or cast off. One of them usually fits my lock and often I have fished my own confiscated key out of the river.

I want out! Mom's voice is a splintery echo against my locked door.

Hush, calm yourself, dearest, you've barely come in, Aunt V says from the talking room into the night. Sleep . . . Rest. . . .

Quicksilver rain bubbles burst on my window pane. Sleep, rest, mom has come back and I know Aunt V will persuade her to rest up at granny-anny's place in the hills, or dry up at NYMPHO'S SACK, as mom would put it. She'll go there. But I shan't come along, not this time, please count me out. Mom and Aunt V and the other sisters are welcome to play their campfire girl games without me or granny-anny. For I'll be far away, I hope. And granny-anny is dead. I'm sure they buried her in the silo, though Aunt V says, nonsense, mama's been laid to rest in the old cemetery next to the old folks home.

She even took me there to show me the gravestone. But I looked the other way.

The weeds were standing high in the silver heat. I raised my eyes and saw an old man swing in a swing from an old tree outside the old folks home. His silver head was flying above the porch roof and his felt slippers seemed to be grazing the tombstones that stretched gray and black into the yellow marshes. I wandered off past the graves to the edge of the marsh and picked the flags that grow wild there for miles. Blue flags. I meant to take them back to the city for Uncle D. But they didn't last through the night. The petals curled up shriveled and glassy-brown like the fingers of a newborn baby, I thought, curling my own fingers.

I told Uncle D about the flags and the grave and the old man in the swing. I tried to talk him into driving with us into the hills. It might make Olli jealous. Besides, it was about time we had a man for a weekend guest, a real man. But Uncle D said he would have to stay in the city. He was allergic to the country, the shrubbery, the grass, the flowers, and yes, even his late mother's azaleas would make him break out into hives, he remembered, sneezing and passing a hand over his face.

Just think of it — an old people's home next door to the cemetery! he exclaimed.

No, he wasn't likely to visit us in the country, and we were stuck with the sisters, the usual crowd whom we'd pick up piecemeal on that slow drive through the worst traffic jam. Each weekend we planned to leave early. But we always left late. Always something was sure to delay us—either mom was sleeping late or she hadn't even come home yet, from an all night poker game god knows where. Or Aunt V herself might be detained at the office, unable to shake off a pig-headed client who refused to take her word for it that the boarded-up house on our alley was not for sale.

A computer salesman, a husband and father with a Tudor style two car garage home in Chappaqua, Aunt V says stiffly from behind the wheel as we are honking and inching our way through the traffic bumper to bumper in our minibus or station wagon Zeroville, a late, late model guaranteed to pollute or your money refunded. Doesn't it strike you as odd, says Aunt V (passing through a red light) that a man of his type should have his heart set on a con-demned house? Unless of course it isn't the house he is after?

Her breath, blowing into my face, smells hot and bitter of black coffee as she is trying to reach mom whose head is hanging out of the open window. I'm squeezed in between them in my new tent dress printed with red poppies. Will you please turn that horrid transistor off, Aunt V says to me. And then, addressing mom again, she says, a beefy type, you may remember him from BANGS. He is the john who couldn't take his eyes off you and that foul smelling waitress.

Why don't you shove it, mom says shortly. And as she bends toward us I see the poppies on my dress reflected in her dark shades.

We creep along at a snail's pace and the only time we are able to pick up speed is when Aunt V passes through another red light. We'll never get to see granny-anny, I say. And Aunt V, already upset enough by mom and the traffic, lifts a hand as though to slap me, and shouts: Will you please get it into your thick head once and for all that my mother has passed on!

Passed on and away. Taken. Gone. Departed—where to? Never say die, says Aunt V. God, how I hate her on those senseless drives through all the boroughs, with countless stops, endless delays, wrong turns as we pick up our weekend guests the sisters from A to Z. They aren't my sisters. They pile into the back of the car, bursting with energy, equipped for the cross country hike they won't be undertaking, the ocean they won't be sailing, the football game they aren't likely to play under the old plum tree. And just as we think we have gotten them all together, one turns out to be still missing after all.

Who's missing?

Q's missing.

Back to Brooklyn Heights, mom commands.

But if Q's missing, T must be missing too. Q + T = 2. Aunt V, turning on mom with open hostility, points out that Q will be riding up with T as usual on T's motorbike.

Back to Brooklyn Heights, I said, says mom.

(From the wild chatter of the sisters in the back Aunt V learns to her unconcealed disgust (UGH!) that Q will ride with us into the hills, as T won't join us till Sunday, because of an unforeseen death.)

I wonder who died. But nobody tells me. Nobody seems to know. Aunt V drives as directed, in tight-lipped silence as mom displays an unexpected familiarity with Q's neighborhood. Turn left a block after the three-way light. Her house is the last on the deadend street to the right. Easy now. There we are. There she is.

Up in the highest turret window of a German story book castle made in Brooklyn sat Princess Q drying her golden hair. Just washed it again, sisters, I won't be long, had a long chat with dad long distance from Boonsville, Mo. He asked me what to preach in church tomorrow morning. I said, preach on love, dad, on love . . .

Q waves at us with her long red hair in the clouds, her tiny boobs bouncing like rubber balls. Mom's looking down at a yellow dog in the street. Then Q's face disappears and now mom looks up at the empty window in the gingerbread turret.

(Behind us the sisters say that Q washes her hair sometimes as often as three or four times a day.)

Aunt V, releasing the emergency brake, announces that she will not wait another minute and that Q is welcome to take the bus.

You'll wait, mom says, putting a heavy hand on Aunt V's shoulder while she continues to stare up to that empty window. But when Q comes finally floating out through the castle or cloister doors barefoot and dressed for the Arabian nights in silky green transparent stuff which wraps around each leg and ties between them, mom doesn't give her so much as a look.

But Aunt V is looking. Her knuckles are white. She clutches the wheel as Q flutters into the back of the car and light as bird onto the maternal lap of a sister. But wait! An inch of her mystery pantaloons gets caught in the door. Hold it! she cries—a signal for Aunt V to back up instantly smack into a battery of garbage cans.

A rip in Q's pantaloons. The deadend street strewn with garbage. (The sanitation workers are on strike.) I laugh up my poppy dress sleeve as irate tenants scream from Gothic windows. A Great Dane (who has been trying unsuccessfully to make it with a tiny Pekinese bitch) jumps high and bares his fangs at old Aunt V. He's racing her. And now she really steps on the gas, pursued for half a mile by his indignant barks which soon are echoed by every dog in the vicinity. So we drive out of Q's borough and toward the hills to the beat of a canine combo.

Arf arf. O what a lovely summer day.

Indian summer. The sky is in mom's dark glasses. Behind her, Q's wet hair flaps in the breeze. She says: Do I miss the army? I do and I don't. It was a love-hate situation between the WACs and me. Too many extroverts in my battalion. But I adored the Heidelberg Schloss, the ruins. I loved the Fass.

She suddenly starts to giggle. The giggles come dropping fast one after the other like glass beads off a broken necklace. CAN'T STOP! Her little tits bounce under the flimsy green stuff, her head bobs forward and onto mom's shoulder. Mom doesn't turn around, but she has reached back and is stroking the head of the convulsed princess.

Stoned again! Aunt V, swinging into the wrong lane and almost colliding with a bloodmobile, announces for all to hear that Q is stoned out of her mind as usual. Stoned blind. Destroyed. Disgusting. Will somebody hand me a stick of gum, please.

Sticks and stones. Q has slipped me a box of candy gift-wrapped for last year's Christmas. I prick my finger on the holly (one drop of blood on my white petticoat) as I tear off the paper, already smelling the sticky sweet smell from inside the box which is printed with poppies as red as the ones on my dress.

Turkish delight. My favorite. Q still has the giggles. She meant to send it as a Christmas gift to granny-anny, but for some unholy reason could not find the post office.

It's just as well you didn't. Mother had already passed on, Aunt V says unfeelingly, and now Q sobs on mom's shoulder to break my heart, dead, dead, sweet little old granny-anny laid to eternal rest, and why hadn't somebody told her, why did everyone including T always try to protect her, pretending there was no death, there only was paradise even in Arabic?

The giggles have dissolved in floods of tears which trickle and vanish in the Sahara sand where she and T will go native, disguised as two sheiks, on one camel. (T, formerly with the Peace Corps in Saudi Arabia, is teaching her Arabic fundamentals from Q to T.)

The Turkish delight is powdered with sugar. I lick it off, I break each little square apart to see if it's a pink or a green one. They are chewy, some taste of perfumed almonds and stick to my teeth, I feel the roof of my mouth with my tongue and think of granny-anny's many chambered cellar, her jam pots high on the shelves. I can't wait to get into the hills and talk to her in my head in the cellar and taste her jams.

Your daughter is making herself sick again, gobbling up all that horrid candy, Aunt V says to mom.

But mom is looking at the sky which is filling out with the hills in big slashes of orange and yellow. Red apples roll from a roadside stand into the road. They roll across the sky in mom's dark shades. Soon we shall see the silo and granny-anny.

From the balls of montezuma . . .the sisters are singing as we are rattling across a bridge. I don't know what's below me, ravine or river. I look straight ahead at the winding dirt road and then sideways at mom to watch for granny-anny's silo in mom's dark, dusty shades.

PAVE PATIO. PAINT FLAGPOLE. DRAIN POOL. Clean. Rake, chop, burn. Dig? Aunt V, licking sharp tip of tiny pencil, adds further items to country chore list: Q??? T

AWL. KEYS! CHECK MORNING GLORIES, BURGLAR
ALARM, SCALES.

The morning glories she intends to check aren't flowers.
They are the in-or-outlets for the pool and they clog up not
only with fallen leaves. Once granny-anny pulled a dead
baby from one of the morning glories. When I heard about
it through the wall I cried all night.

Of course Aunt V will be checking the bathroom scales
because she suspects me of having rigged them again to
show my weight 30 pds lighter. Amen. Next time I'll smash
those scales. Nobody's going to tell me to work off my fat.
I'm not her slave. Let her do her own dirty work. She and
the sisters, they love to work till they drop.

They shovel, dig, and rake and scrub and paint. They lug
and hammer. Granny-anny's place sounds like a construc-
tion site in lower Manhattan. Weekend spells work without
end. Most of the sisters, all of them maybe (but count out Q)
are rearing to flex their muscles. They say: All week in the
city we've been sitting on our asses like so many JC's riding
into Jerusalem. So get to it, sisters! Drop your cocks and
grab your socks as we say in the navy. (Yes, man, confides
V2 to V, I too rose from the WAVES like Venus. Wait till
you see my tattoo.)

OK, shake ass! Shoulder your spades, sisters! Wir sind die
Moorsoldaten. . . . Drag wheelbarrows and pickaxes out of
the old tool shed. The patio cries to be repaved. It's all torn
up. A mile or so behind the blabber brook is an abandoned
quarry. We'll haul the rocks from there and split them to fit
V's V-shaped patio under the crazy plum tree.

Sweat the city poisons out of your system and pump the
quarry dust into your lungs. Sore mother muscles make for
pleasure moans of pain through toil. (Man, I can hardly
stand up!) When the sun slips down behind the wooded

hills, we'll put the tools away and line up for a sauna bath or soak luxuriously like Cleopatra in Rubinstein's mother milk pour le bain No. 5. (Please rub me down with Johnson's baby oil.) Now change into clean clothes and down we troop for cocktails and dinner by candlelight and slow close dancing in the grass to Schubert's DEATH & THE MAIDEN.

The record is playing now though it is early afternoon and no one would dream of dancing. No one, except Q, that is. Oh, my aching back! Aunt V, crouching in the chrysanthemums, moans long and loud so mom should hear. I'm sick of Q's Shoobird, she adds with a hiss through the mums.

But mom, drinking slivovitz from granny-anny's earthen jug, has stoppled her ears. And Q hears only the five fiddlers in DEATH & THE MAIDEN, if she can still hear anything. She is tripping on the torn-up patio in harem pants, with vine leaves in her hair and a wire basket swinging from the crook of her arm. The wind shakes the plums from the tree and she picks them up carefully one by one and drops them into the basket where they slip right through the wire mesh and back onto the ground. O wild wild death, she hums with a spaced-out smile.

Mom, legs crossed under her, is sitting on an upended rain barrel. I wonder is she watching Q? It's hard to tell because her eyes are hidden behind the dark shades and all I can see in the shades are the falling plums.

The delivery truck is crawling blue along the blue horizon and I wave with both arms, hoping that Olli will see me. I climb up the ladder that's leaning against the silo. But I don't see him, I see his big brother who is driving because Olli hasn't got his license yet. He is too young. He says it burns him up that he has to deliver the groceries from his dad's store while brother has all the fun, driving, munching the candy bars he'd steal by the fistful from under his dad's counter, or blowing a stolen condom into a balloon.

The sun is a yellow balloon in the white sky. For a second I think that Olli is waving at me, and I begin to feel hot and wet under my poppy dress. But then I realize it's the American flag atop the antenna that has been waving at me from the truck. So I climb down the ladder. The bottom rung cracks as I jump into the grass. And Q who has been standing at the foot of the ladder, painting a circle of miniature hearts on the silo, cries: T! is it U?—and drops the can of red paint. It spills on the grass.

We've painted our garden red, sings Q. And she stretches out in the grass alongside the red puddle and goes to sleep.

Mom too is asleep, upstairs in the bathtub where she passed out an hour ago behind the drawn yellow shades. Aunt V has left by army jeep to pick up the groceries (no Olli for me until night?) and the sisters are still splitting rocks. There is a veiled moon in the sky though it is daytime. Will it rain? I climb down into the dark basement to check out the jam pots. But the old woman who pretends to be granny-anny has gotten there ahead of me. Aunt V says she hired her to look after the house though I know she is being paid to spy on me, and she is wearing all of granny-anny's old clothes, even the long black shawl.

You'll never fool me! I tell her. But she doesn't even look up from under the knitted shawl. She keeps counting the jam pots. You are not granny-anny! I say and slam the cellar door shut and climb the steep narrow stairway to granny-anny's old room under the slanting roof. There I used to

sleep on a cot next to her postered bed. But now that bed
has become my bed and my skin is beginning to smell like
hers, of rain and slivovitz and wool and Turkish delight.
And if I'm in the mood for it in the rain I can dream in
Croatian under a cloud of goose feathers.

Shut the shutters and you make your own night, you
make the three halos on the ikon glow green over the bed,
and the seven red hearts on the treasure chest under the
window glow white and red. Her life was stored inside that
chest, granny-anny used to tell me and I believed her because I was little then. Besides she always kept the chest
locked and the key hidden. But now the lid is always open
and I can sit in front of it on the waxed floor and rummage
through odds and ends of her past though her real life must
be stored away elsewhere, perhaps in the silo. I can rummage among those multicolored skeins of wool from which
she meant to knit me a sweater, and yes, it's the incomplete
items inside the chest that give me the oddest feeling, as
though she might be standing over me this minute to pick
up from where she had stopped, stitch a face on my rag doll
for Christmas or darn the gray wool stocking whose heel she
has already stuffed with the darning egg. A painted,
brightly lacquered wooden egg made to resemble a peasant
girl, maybe granny-anny herself in her Sunday apron. You
twist it open at the waist and out flutter two folded tickets
for the circus, unused and stamped with a lost date, Dec. 11,
1910. Matinée.

Dried milkweed pods. An empty match box. Spools of
lavender thread, and wrapped in a piece of red flannel the
plastic hearing aid she rarely used. I use it to deafen the
noise when the sisters carry on too late into the night or
morning with DEATH & THE MAIDEN. It does away with
outside noises as it crackles and sputters inside my ear like

my little transistor. That hearing aid too is part of her unfinished past, like the unfinished letter which reads, DEAR BR and then stops dead for all eternity, as I do not really believe that she'll bother with any of those items again. My sweater will remain unknitted, her stocking undarned, and her dead husband's egg-shaped, chocolate colored photo will never be framed. For years she had planned to put him into a frame and in fact whenever I'd hear her mention him it would be in connection with that frame she was going to buy to show off his brave handsome face, she might say, though as far as I could make out from the picture he had no more of a face than my unfinished rag doll. And didn't Aunt V insist that her father had been a faceless man, a weak man who had thought nothing of letting his wife support him, just like her own J's or X's had depended on V for support? Huh, men! she'd say with a singular hate when granny-anny would talk of the silver frame she was going to get for her fine young man who died in his prime of TB.

My faceless grandad. He still is waiting for his silver frame as he leans, mustached and limp, against a potted palm below the photographer's gilded signature in Croatian. I lick his chocolate face and put him away with other unfinished business—a skirt half basted, glass beads to be strung up for a rosary, a check to be signed.

A tiny empty bottle. Moth balls. Black tissue paper. And folded lengthwise inside a pencil box, addressed to whom it may concern, a letter commending granny-anny for her long and loyal service as house maid and cook for the A. C. Lavenders in Mystic, Connecticut.

The sisters are taking turns riding the power mower up

and down the bumpy lawn to DEATH & THE MAIDEN. But I don't hear them. I have tuned in on granny-anny's hearing aid which makes its own noise. Snap pop & crackle: it's carrying on in my head the way granny-anny said it used to in hers to the exclusion of all other sounds and often so loud she'd fear she might turn stone deaf. She said her daughter was a fool to believe that the gadget would help her hear more, and if she gave in and wore it at all it simply was to keep the peace between them or whatever little peace they had, she might add. For they were in each other's hair every day, largely because granny-anny kept trying to convince her that she should remarry one of her old X's and produce a whole lot of new little j's. Yes, once or twice she had even contrived to invite either Jock or Jake to the house over the weekend and I think it was mom who locked them up in the silo.

No, granny-anny never had her wish for many grandchildren come true, I was slated to be an only grandchild, and as for Aunt V's brother, big W, he wasn't likely to make babies at his age. He was too lazy, granny-anny supposed, though he was a gifted musician and played the accordion for free meals and handouts at a Croatian saloon on Ave A. She had gone there once, but never again. The food they served wasn't fit for a pig. It stank and she wouldn't have bothered to travel to the city if the hearing aid hadn't played one of its tricks on her and advised her to go.

For that gadget had from the first talked with a voice of its own, as if an invisible devil were living inside it, crackling, cackling, planting sinful thoughts in her head, spreading ungodly lies. Still she tried her best to get used to it and it was plugged into her ear that clammy morning when she and I were walking back from the p.o. where she had picked up her weekly Croatian paper. We were taking the short-cut through the milkweed in a gray drizzle, past the blighted pear tree hung with a few rotting pears, when that old guy in his long World War I army coat stepped up to us like out of nowhere.

But that was how he had appeared before—like out of nowhere. I'd walk by the pear tree alone, and suddenly he'd be there. I still don't know what scared me more, his face which was like a half eaten pear, with one of his cheeks missing; or his wearing nothing under the army coat. He'd flip it open, pretending he meant to urinate by the pear tree when he really meant to have me look at his dick, a gray, shriveled thing which reminded me of the deflated arm of my rubber doll, the one I used to fondle in the tub when I was little.

But on that drizzly morning he did not show it to me. His ancient military coat was buttoned up to the chin and down to the knees. He stepped right up to granny-anny and said, excuse me, madam, but I thought you'd better know: your daughter is a woman lover.

Granny-anny looked puzzled. What? What? she asked him although he had already disappeared in the drizzle. Why don't you leave me alone? she said into the amplifier in a weak voice. But then she stamped her foot and spit on the ground, and jerking the plug out of her ear she cursed the hearing aid for having pestered her with stupid lies just once too often. You nasty little devil, you! We're through! And she made as if she were hurling the gadget into the milkweed although in a second she had thrust it into her black scratched-up old purse.

She wouldn't take me by the hand as we turned to walk

back home. You run ahead, she said. I want to think. And it wasn't till an hour later that she came home soaking wet and with her coat muddied, maybe because she had been sitting in the open field. Aunt V was shouting from the porch that Olli had once again delivered the wrong box of groceries (he asked could he take B to the school dance but I told him she was too young to be dating and so was he!) and that the country fresh eggs they'd had for breakfast had been rotten again.

Don't you hear me? You are the one who keeps ordering those eggs, she said as granny-anny looked at her uncomprehendingly. Please use your hearing aid, mama!

But granny-anny shrugged and said *gluv* which meant deaf in the old country.

Gluv, Gluv. Now she was in the kitchen, flouring the top of the old wooden table on which to roll out the pastry dough which she would let me help her cut into circles and spread with ruby red jams and shape into pockets. She let me eat right from the jam pot while the pastry was in the oven. But she wasn't saying anything except *gluv gluv*. And later at dinner she would not sit down with the rest of us but insisted on standing and serving as though she were still a hired maid in the Lavender's household in Mystic. She carried a folded napkin over one arm, and each time she changed the plates or poured out the wine she bowed and murmured pardon me, madam, even to her own daughter.

The sisters begged her to sit down with them. But granny-anny said *gluv*. Aunt V looked either angry or embarrassed. She was playing with her knife. It slipped out of her hand and onto the floor with an odd vibrating twang as from a tuning fork. Damn, she said, stooping to pick it up. But granny-anny had already picked it up and their heads collided under the table.

For Pete's sake, mama! Cut it out! Aunt V had blushed.
Sit down and eat! she said, pointing the knife at granny-
anny's empty chair at the head of the long table. But
granny-anny had shuffled off to the kitchen.

Aunt V whispered, I'm afraid she is getting senile. She
tapped the edge of the knife to the glass as though she
wanted to make a formal announcement, while the sisters,
glum and embarrassed, were picking at their food.

It was the same story at supper. Again she wouldn't share
the meal with us. And each time before entering with a
fresh supply of muffins under the napkin (on which it said
in cross-stitch HOME SWEET HOME) she would knock at
the door although it stood wide open.

The rain was coming down in sheets that night. Aunt V
had built a fire in the fun room and plugged in the record
player and rolled up the rugs so everyone could have a ball
and dance or wrestle. But I stayed in the kitchen with
granny-anny. She had slammed the door shut and sat down
at the big old table with a bottle of slivovitz while I was
setting up the board for our nightly game of monopoly,
eager as always to make another killing in imaginary real
estate just as Aunt V would in real life. I usually won at that
game. For even if I made some poor investments granny-
anny was sure to make worse ones.

But tonight she played a sharp game, and she was wide
awake, even though she kept drinking slivovitz, the way
mom likes to drink, right from the bottle. It didn't look right
on granny-anny. But everything was upside down tonight,
especially our game. She kept winning and winning. She

really was cleaning me out. Her face was disappearing fast behind green heaps of make-believe money and when it re-emerged into the light it no longer looked like her face. For she had removed her false teeth. And as she tilted her head back and opened her mouth to drink from the bottle I found myself staring into an empty tunnel. Her eyes were two empty tunnels. Her cheeks had caved in and her straggly hair and whiskers had turned into bits of grass under the greenshaded ceiling lamp which was swinging back and forth to the beat of the rain and the wind.

And she kept winning. I remember the rush of the wind in the chimney as she was grabbing my last hotel, not saying a word. And after another swig from the bottle (the empty tunnel of her mouth glowed red) she grabbed up all the remaining country clubs and three banks as well as the Santa Fe railroad and the boardwalk of Atlantic City.

For the first time in my life I hated her and I think I told her aloud that she looked like a witch though I can't be sure I really said it as I could not hear my own words in the sudden commotion. The wind had blown the door open and was blowing the make-believe money in all directions as a Scottish reel came blaring from the fun room where the sisters were dancing and stomping and clapping their hands.

But granny-anny too was clapping her hands and in a moment she was on her feet and inside the fun room where the electric light had been switched off and the only light there was came from that big red fire Aunt V had built in the fireplace to last through the night.

gluv gluv. Granny-anny was stamping to the dizzy music and grinning with her toothless gums showing battered and gray. She had pulled her long black skirt up over her head like a hood and her naked, wrinkled backside too was gray like her stockings which were formless as though she had stuffed them with old rags. And altogether she looked gray and tattered like the old rag doll she had started to make and then had left outside in the rain unfinished.

Gluv gluv, she kept saying or chanting as the record went on and on. More hopping than limping (for the slivovitz must have deadened her arthritic aches) she had moved closer to the fire and now her gray skin became alive with pink and red lights. And the sisters who had been dancing in pairs or alone fled toward the wall into the shadows as granny-anny was sticking out her bare ass at them, gluv gluv, bending down as far as her stiff joints would let her before she started to dance around and around in the middle of the floor against the spluttering fire.

Stop it, mama! Aunt V had jumped up from the couch where she had been lying in the shadows invisibly, with her head in mom's lap. (Mom had passed out of course. Mom was asleep.)

Stop it, mama! Aunt V had lunged forward, had pulled granny-anny's skirt down and grabbed her elbow to take her away. But granny-anny refused to budge. For a scary second she stared at her daughter (still with that toothless grin) and then she shook herself free and slapped her across the face hard back and forth with the back of her big-knuckled hand.

Aunt V was sitting on the floor with a nose bleed, crying like a baby as the sisters hovered about her with paper napkins, handkerchiefs and ice cubes. But granny-anny (as if the night were just another night in the fun room) got busy with those minor chores she'd perform before saying goodnight: She emptied ashtrays, picked up empty bottles and cans from the floor and threw another log on the fire. Then she opened the window to let out the smoke.

The rain had stopped. The night was hanging cool and still in the window, with a string of stars in the tree like a thin icicle. I think I heard a fox, and from above granny-anny's slow, heavy footfall.

Someone (mom?) has thrown white paint at the silo. The QT hearts have disappeared and only one arrow remains. Q has washed her hair and stuck her head into the rain barrel for a rinse, rain turning hair softer than silk as it is made by weeping angels, she says to T who has arrived on her motorbike directly from the funeral service. (We still don't know who died. Maybe she killed a man, says mom, spitting tobacco juice from an upstairs window.)

Princess Q in the grass in the sun, drying her rain-rinsed hair. Smells sweeter than it does in Brooklyn where she uses a vinegar rinse and the yolk of a duck egg. Eier & Essig, Rapunzel remembers from her waggish Heidelberg WAC days. But no, says T, it's Arabic we have to study. She is crouching at Q's feet like a fat horny toad. But she is a gentle toad. She gently picks up Q's dainty foot and begins to enamel the tiny toe nails with silver polish. Each toe nail a miniature ikon. I'll never forget, says T with a gentle laugh, how you wrapped me up in your long hair when we had our first go five thousand years ago at MOTHER HUB-BARD'S.

Oh not that long ago, coos Q.

A pigeon flirting with a toad. How long ago since they decided to save the disability checks from the WACS to finance their adventure into the Arabian nights? They'd traverse the sandy waste prosperously in the guise of two improbable sheiks, one fat, one thin as a sparrow. Each month they plan to leave the following month. They are still here, still planning to save and travel.

We must learn to save our money, says T and she plants a kiss on the sole of Q's neat little foot.

Please tickle my feet with a grass blade, says Q. Please, now, T, tickle me, it turns me on.

Shit, mom says into the wind. She clears her throat and spits tobacco juice from that upstairs window where she is sitting wedged into the frame, with the bathroom curtains billowing orange and yellow above her head, and her knees hugged to her chest. Her sneakers are splashed with white paint. She knocks the ashes out of the pipe and raps the pipe bowl against the ledge. But neither Q nor T appear to notice. T has found the tail feather of a crow and now she is busy tickling Q's feet, Q giving off weak little shrieks and giggles as she lies back in the grass, with her heels on T's fleshy thighs though in their heads of course they are both riding through the desert on a camel.

Hoho! Mom has started a new pipe and is blowing smoke circles into the sky for Q to admire. But Q's face is under her hair as under a veil. Our pilgrimage will lead us where? she asks through the veil. Maybe I ought to stain my skin with walnut juice so I can pass as a boy. Because I want to pray with you in those mosques we've been reading about in the travel folders. Do you think you can grow a beard?

T says she can try.

Q, wiggling her feet, discloses that her clergyman dad sent her a small check after she had told him on the phone long distance how she and another single Methodist girl were planning to do missionary work for a year in Saudi Arabia.

Now what do you say to that!

T says nothing, absorbed as she is in her task of tickling the unreal feet of her princess.

We'll make a team like the late Burtons, Sir R and his sainted I, Q chants exaltedly. But then she is overcome by the giggles again (Stop it, T! Stop it!), and T stops at once and pulls her up ever so gently and in a moment she has hoisted her onto her shoulders and is trotting off through the weeds, with Q's mane flying and a lone buzzard circling in the spent blue high above.

Aunt V, crossing the lawn with a spray gun, stops short and calls up to the bathroom window, isn't it simply marvelous, J, how the two keep loving each other? Though mom has already disappeared from the window and Q and T have disappeared into the woods.

Mom in the bathtub, asleep. Siesta time for nearly everyone, but Aunt V wide awake atop a ladder, smoking out a wasp nest at the back of the house. She is wearing the gas mask she saved from her WWII CD days as the air raid warden, sector commander, BANGS DISTRICT.

Somebody's playing Q's DEATH & THE MAIDEN, that record I hate, old Mr. Bones chasing some poor little maiden or maybe me down to the grave, I hate that, god knows what Q sees in it or hears, I don't, I've smashed the record I won't tell you how often and each time it's resurrected, I swear, with the same scratch on the same note exactly. Tot, tod or toad: I flee through scatter clumps of scarlet dahlias, away from the back of the house which juts out broad and bare like granny-anny's when she turned it to them in the firelight and told them in Croatian to kiss it.

Shoo bird. I thumb my nose at old bones and Aunt V behind her smokescreen. She can't see through it, she can think what she likes, that I am raking up the leaves before they rot or reading Oliver Twist or doing push-ups. Forget it. What does she know? She won't know where I'm going or that I'm with granny-anny this minute, now, even as I climb the fence on my way to the dumps. There she sits, always under the same old tree, always knitting on the same long shawl to cover the earth. Her stockings are sagging. They've fallen down to her swollen ankles and I may contemplate with her the geography of her legs, those bulging veins like rivers amid smooth valleys.

(Here in this valley, between two streams, she says pointing, was the monastery where the bearded monks let you drink from the well to cure many ailments such as gout, goiters and varicose veins.)

Her long black shawl drifts backward to the sky like smoke as I run away from home, each time for ever. For ever is never, each time I stumble over the same looped root and the same fallen bird nest.

Tired little old butterfly hanging on to a milkweed stalk. Too weak to fly off, even as Olli comes creeping up on me from out of the bushes to scare me, he does it each time. He has been selling fish. I can tell by the smell. He has the longest legs, the reddest hair. His big toe sticks through his sneaker. Daddy-long-legs comes scurrying across a tuft of moss and he tries to crush my favorite spiderman under his sneaker, but fails and so he laughs, jumps up my back and cries, Where shall I put the groceries, ma'm?

The usual place, I say.

It is an old joke between us. He first said it when he pulled up in his father's pick-up truck with the groceries for Aunt V. Where to put it in the beautiful weeds where dwarf colonels stand in tufts like pert little nosegays. Skunk cabbage too and they smell sweet to me. We always fuck in the same spot, standing up and in earshot of Aunt V, almost. I call him Olli-tread-lightly or Daddy-go-sweet. Bend down, he says, quick, no time to take it off, just let me squeeze in quick or they'll catch us, we'll be catching whatnot, you and me, no, no, keep standing, quick.

The first time my head was getting so dizzy I didn't know if I was coming to or going where, I nearly dropped, but I kept standing up. (My face on the morning after a mess of red pimples. Aunt V: What happened to my poor baby? Me: It fell into the poison ivy.) Poor baby nothing. Dizzy. He went so fast I went under. Came up to gasp for breath, then drowned for good. He said I was a real cutie.

Aunt V, what if she were to pop up suddenly, maybe to dump garbage unlawfully into the bushes behind her property, what would she do if she caught us making it fast and sweet? Would she do what she once swore (in the talking room to mom in the night rain) she'd do to the first man who'd take advantage of my virgin innocence? She swore she'd tear out his testicles with her bare hands. Balls, mom said into the night rain.

Just let Aunt V try it, let her show up and we'll throw her head first into the poison ivy. The thought makes me laugh like crazy. He says: Shut up! Red hot, he's all the way inside, filling me please make it last, in and out smooth, long, longer till the earth shakes inside my belly. Can't wait, sometimes I grab it from his pants and shake it, sometimes he makes me suck it, I like the fish taste, I don't like the smell, why don't we ever kiss? No time, he says we do it the natural way like the animals, though I wonder how it would be to have him on top slow, slow long into the night. No time, he says. Quick!

(He's slow in school, his dad said to Aunt V in the store by the frozen food counter. Aunt V said slow or quick, what does it matter as long as he's honest. He's never short-changed her yet, fine cleancut allamerican youngster. Has a genius for fitting the groceries into the box so every bit of space is put to good use. Has drive & patience. Presidential material.)

President O, Olli-go-smoothly, god, my juices are piping like birds in the feathered light. Sometimes we make it nights, we did, he shed all over me twice and I let his juice dry on me like fish scales while I was sleeping off my dreams and Uncle D in granny-anny's postered bed. Why don't we strip? I said why don't we, naked? I said let's kiss, he said no time, too risky, kid, he said, my dad, your mom, your aunt. My ass, my O he asked was it true we were running a nudist colony?

Not a word of truth in it, Olli.

Seems a guy named Guy was doing a spray job from his piping red piper plane, was flying low enough to see, he said he ·saw them, guys and chicks, skinny dippers laid out nakedy nude on Japanese straw mats like so many rows of skinned sardines, cross my liver.

The tales they will tell in the village.

Are you kidding? O no O, I don't skinny dip, can't swim, I only go into the pool to drown myself. In granny-anny's navy blue bloomers.

Are you pullin' my leg or something?

Olli's breath hard and fast on the nape of my neck, Quick! His teeth in my wooly hair. NOW! Man, you got hair like a spade, he says, sure your mom didn't make a mistake?

At night all cats are black, I say my dad is dead, my dad I say was a big black died-in-the-wool buccaneer from Little Rock Ark.

You kiddin? He's zipped up his fly. Manly gesture of Olli the Red. Red fuzz on arms and chin. Red lashes, rabbit eyes red, quick as a rabbit. Flash. My moan for more is putting out the sun.

He spits into his hand to slick down his red pompadour while I rub myself under the tent dress. The rusted beer cans, soup cans, the smashed bottles that lie in enchanted heaps in the underbrush begin to hum. Small insects hum in feather clouds and down I flop on a rotting foam mattress somebody, maybe Aunt V, has discarded here. I pat my belly. Do you love me, Olli?

Yeah, sure, you're a real cutie, I better get back on my bike, beat it back to the store. My dad's expecting me back.

Expecting, expecting. Always on the run, my lover, just like my uncle. I slap my hand to my belly. It sounds like a drum. Wait, Olli! What if I told you I was going to have a baby?

What? He wipes his hand against the shiny seat of his pants. Stares at me. Mouth hanging open. Makes him look stupid. WHAT?

A cuddly fuzzy olli dolli baby bear that's what.

I rub and rock on the foam rubber dock. I want.

WHAT? Come again!

Pregnant, stupid!

How come! He kicks a bloody ketchup bottle, breaks its neck. His freckles are swarming all over his face, off into the bushes. What? I mean gee B gee whiz I mean you kiddin!

Cross my womb and hope to fly.

Gee-Zuz! Cross-eyed Olli stammer-stumbles, squirms, puts one hand on the saddle of his second-hand bike. Is ready to take off but can't. Too much of the gentleman. Throat purple and lumpy. Sweats. The fuzz of his almost beard is standing on end. Gee B like I mean like I said like wow like christ like shit!

Kicks the last bloody drops out of that ketchup bottle.

Cuts his big toe. Coo coo Olli Colli watch out there's blood in your shoe. I'm Cinderella.

Yeah . . . Glumly stares down at his bloody big toe that's sticking through his sneaker. Gee B you mean we've been doin you know what I mean like for months without you takin you know what girls do dunno you not goin to do that to me man fuck you if my dad finds out how do you know aint some other kid's baby like you been doin it with other kids. . . .

Yeah! He flexes his arm (exactly like Uncle D) to look at his Timex. Time to get back to the store. So lover Olli rolls down his sleeves and steps behind the tree to piss. His jet arcs crystal clear. Just look at that! Shakes off the last rain drop. Tucks it away. Well B it sure is a bummer though I betcha you made a mistake. Got to be off or Dad is going to beat the shit out of me. Mum's the word. Want to do it again tonight? Midnight. Same spot. Bye now.

Bye and of course the word is Mom. The red tail lights blink as he pedals off down the winding dirt road downhill into nothing. No hands! No feet! Big deal. If he graduates from highschool he may get a motor bike. I squat above his puddle and try to piss too. But nothing comes. I sniff and wait. The spiderweb between two speckled leaves is hung with his dew drops.

The same big fire roars in the chimney in the country parlor fun salon, though granny-anny remains absent. Yes, she must be dead. Mom's lying by the artificial brickwall as good as dead, with her head under a poncho into which rows of little llamas gray as dust are woven in stiff-legged patterns. From deep down in the cellar I can hear Q sing maybe the Lorelei as she imagines herself in a secret underground passage in Heidelberg on the WAC, stoned blind on MJ.

J under her Peruvian poncho does not stir.

How many hours till midnight and should I meet Olli, or should I stand him up and make him wonder? I sit down in the corner under the cuckoo clock. Like granny-anny I'm invisible. Nobody sees me, not even T or Aunt V who have installed themselves in the long, overstuffed sofa in a printed garden of chintz: T doing crewel work while memorizing short Arabic phrases (Thank you for the camel, sir. One room for two.) as Aunt V is wildly digging through the Sunday Times for the classified section. Who burned it? Who chewed it up? Aunt V is clawing through an avalanche of paper. (Too many trees, she sighs, must die to keep us informed.)

But damn it, this is last month's paper! I want today's. The same old headlines week after week. It's rather comforting, though I'm after the classified. I am, she explains (shoving the mass of paper onto the floor with a smart karate chop), hunting for a new secretary. My trusted U has quit.

She wants to be alone in the basement, says T.

Not Q. U, V corrects. Same difference, same color hair, red gold or vice versa, only U wore a wig.

Not Q! cries T.

No, U, says V. She was a secretary to end them all. She was a realtor's dream. Heavens! Why did I say DREAM?

Dream.

Aunt V, leaning back and deeper into her garden of glazed chintz, pale elderberry leaves, ashes of roses, says, yes it was because of a dream that U quit her job, a dream she had while asleep in bed with her Irish sweetheart, an alcoholic freckled youth (male) whom poor old U had been supporting ever since the disappearance or death of her husband, I forget which.

Poor U, built like an aging stripper. But handsome. Straight as an arrow and then some.

Q?

U. Lived in Queens, traveled by subway. Dreamed she was standing (Hear! Hear!) inside the men's room of the Queens Plaza Station IND.

Who?

U. A white-tiled, long and antiseptic lavatory. Clean as death. Not filthy like in a real life MTA situation. Queens tunnel-like it stretched, sterile and holy. And there was U in her so-called pants suit (hand-me-down from her employer V) staring at the backs of a dozen men in identical business suits as they were busy urinating in unison though each into his separate porcelain stall.

I'll B . . .

U R. When they were done they turned to face her, only they had no faces, each head was a white egg and their flies stood open though they showed her nothing either. And U, caught fast in that dream trap which all of us have experienced in our own dreams if not in a real life MTA situation inside a stalled subway train—poor U had the awful suspicion or certainty that each of those faceless, identical businessmen was expecting of her that she unzip her fly and take out her . . .

SCREAM! Aunt V is screaming like a lunatic, causing T to jump and yell, Q! Q!

Down, T. Back to your crewel frame. Your Q is underground and safe, singing ICH WEISS NICHT WAS. Aunt V has merely screamed to illustrate U's waking up alongside her lover who pats her rump with a feeble hand and mumbles (like Olli): You sick or somepin?

The rest, says Aunt V, pouring herself a glass of buttermilk, is history, to be sure.

To be sure, I've heard her tell it to mom nights, how U crawled out of bed over her lover's insensitive body, he having fallen asleep again, maybe into his own Queens Plaza subway nightmare; how U put on that same pinstriped pants suit (hand-me-down from V, remember) and a shoulderlength Q-red wig, and false lashes, lipstick and rouge to betake herself to the nearest Queens bar for transvestites and men in leather. No ladies invited.

U, drenched in Shalimar, steps to the bar and in a husky whiskey voice through which rings that southern drawl, she squeezes in between two leatheroos and orders a double scotch. Bottoms up. U like Uncle D speaks with two different voices. Ding dong dell, southern bell U in the witching well, bewitching the sturdy men folks. Another drinkie winkie dear? Don't mind if I do, darling. But gentlemen, no pawing please. Keep your hands to yourself, in their usual place. My name is Yukatan and I'm a lady.

Outqueening every single queen in the saloon. Would you believe it?

Believe you me, V tattles to J or T, U had the toughies eat out of her hand and they loved it. She had them totally convinced that she was a he in drag. Seems some of the q's were jealous, they picked a fight and one tore off U's wig and the other grabbed what should have been falsies, ready to tear that out too. Only it was the real thing.

Real tits and you better believe it, V titters to T in the chintz over a Schlitz.

Hold everything!

No sooner had the leather boys been alerted that a female had sneaked into the exclusive club under the guise of a male disguised as a broad than the blank hit the fan and she was beaten something awful. Was clubbed and kicked and tossed out with a broken nose into the suburban night street known as the other boulevard of broken hopes.

Might have died there had not a kindly ambulance driver spotted her and delivered her to the psycho ward of the nearest Veteran hospital.

Question: Is a broken nose sufficient to qualify for psychiatric care?

Answer: Not normally, unless you keep insisting like U that you are a veteran male homosexual transvestite.

Get me out of here! Get me out! Q cries from the lower depth, the musty basement. (Someone, it seems, has locked the cellar door and lost the key.)

Cuckoo. Above my head the door in the clock has snapped open and the repulsive little bird pecks at the night. Count the cuckoos. High time for my night date behind the garbage with Olli. Am mad for you, Olli, no matter what, whether we make it standing or falling.

Good grief! The child's still up! Aunt V exclaims, having noticed me only this moment.

Cuckoo. I've already slipped upstairs, into granny-anny's room or mine. The stars are skating in the sky and through my head. That dummy I've made from a blanket and rags and things: she'll be taking my place in bed while I am rolling through the stars with Olli. Aunt V will be busy for hours to come, trying to find the key to the cellar door. And should mom come to my room (but she never does) she won't know it's the dummy she is kissing good night.

No, I will never go to the country with them again. They're welcome to take my dummy instead. She lost the seven pounds I gained. I weighed us both. I'm finished with the hills and granny-anny has danced her last jig by the fire. Like Olli, I'm through with him too, he couldn't care less if he made it with me or the dummy. I don't think he looked at my face once, thanks. He never shows his face when he gets to the city to baby-sit for one of his seven sisters. I baby-sit with my transistor. The rain is making waves around the moon.

Sound waves. The latest lunar bulletin. We're short of oxygen. The flag don't breathe. I breathe. I listen inside out of me for ripples of sound. But from the talking room below not a squeak. Mom's most recent flight and capture has left her with nothing to say. Her face, a silent, disembodied moon floats on the night waves like my swollen belly. I run my palm across it in a circle. Behind me three bloodless months. I have been checking off the days on the calendar the way Aunt V checked off each day that mom was missing. Her calendar sits by her bed, but mine hangs on the wall, with MC COFFREY'S FOODSTORE FREE DELIVERY printed on it above a picture of Old Glory.

Was it possible, I asked Uncle D in C Park, for a girl my age to go through her change of life? He understood me wrong, thought deep and hard. He put a finger to his nose and sighed before he said life meant perpetual change at any age from the womb to the tomb, and yes this very second momentous changes were occurring inside and around us, chemical evolutions or dissolutions. It was a matter of semantics. It was a dream.

Vita somnium breve. He wrote it down for me on the back of a lavender envelope addressed not to him but to a Monsieur de D, Roma, fermo in posta. How had it gotten into his safari pocket? he asked, unfolding a laundry fresh handkerchief, lavender too and embroidered with a black J.

More mysteries. Mixed in with last week's laundry, his pillow slips, he had found a sheer nightgown trimmed with black lace. Life was a dream, short or long, and he mustn't, he said, forget to question his Chinese laundryman, or rather the man's son, an MIT drop out and designer of fine lingerie.

VSB. I slipped the envelope into my pocket. And I pinched myself to make sure our sitting there on the Central Park rock in the Sunday sun was not a dream. I pinched myself so hard I winced. I still have a blue mark on my arm.

Please D, take B off my hands for the day, Aunt V had wailed that Sunday over the phone as she had stood deserted in her gray body stocking in the gray morning, gray-faced for want of sleep. Her mother has deserted her! she had cried, shocked and incredulous, as though this never had happened before. But of course mom never had been absent for such a very long time before and Aunt V's calendar showed more absence marks than lunar cycles.

No, D, Aunt V said into the phone, J wasn't drunker than usual, in fact she may have been more sober, didn't even slam the door or cuss, just gave me the slip, no message whatever, and god she left her keys under the welcome mat. O D! cried V, she was my child, my sister, put them together and they spell mother, my therapist's nailed the trouble down to the fact that I was breast fed too long and she not at all. What do you suggest I do, D?

Do D, I listened in on my extension princess style. Uncle D murmured condolences, using his southern voice. Poor trusting V. But surely, the dichotomy, he murmured, would not last for ever, though it might reoccur of course unless J was kept under lock and key. Closely watched day and night. Behind bars.

The zoo should amuse her. I'm speaking of B, said Aunt V. The exercise should do her good. She likes you, D, but don't let her nag you. Cakes, cokes, malts, tarts and splits are strictly verboten. O D! My J's gone over the hill. I'm dying of anguish.

Aunt V's protracted death. Mom's gin bottles gathered dust. The kidney shaped bar in the talking room was a deserted altar of double mirrors.

Talk talk. For days and nights Aunt V had been hanging on the phone in search of a clue as to mom's whereabouts; answering countless calls: berating the computer in Ashland for giving her Phoenix; dialing from coast to coast and ship to shore. The sisters have a nation-wide underground network but the wires get crossed too often and the Mystic operator speaks with the voice of Creve Coeur.

Hurricanes, twisters, blizzards and sand-storms swooshed through my extension phone as Aunt V chased after mom's footprints, fingerprints, a T-shirt with the laundry mark ripped out, a short blond hair in the soup. U.S. United Sisterhood. Your J, guessed K in L.A., must have taken off with my doll. My car has disappeared. So has my checkbook. The pair was last seen in St. Joe, patron of cuckolded husbands, forgive me V, I'm high as a kite, am merely guessing, guess Q should know a thing or two. Hang on. I'll find you her number . . .

A needless reminder. Stab in the wounded heart. Aunt V knew Q's number by heart, having dialed it a hundred times. Each time T answered for Q, ominously, thought Aunt V. T told her that she was holding the fort in Brooklyn while Q was with her clergyman dad in Boonsville, Mo, hoping to squeeze a fat check out of the old fool to speed up their long-delayed departure for Arabia.

Her Q, said trusting T, was true as gold. To which Aunt V, trembling with jealousy, replied that she had no faith in the gold standard. Click went the receiver. The dial was spinning again, the wires were singing. She tried for a connection with Boonsville, but reached Washington D.C. instead, another clergyman there who was nobody's father. Her Valencienne lace hankie was chewed to shreds when finally she landed with the right party, Q's reverend dad.

Of course, my dear lady! he boomed in a voice full of cheer and religion. Of course J is at my house, he always was and will be, hopefully for evermore, a steady welcome guest at our table, he is at your table if you believe in him, seek and ye shall find, he's never far. May I suggest a selection of bible readings?

Aunt V gasped for air, cried Jesus!, and dropped the receiver.

Drops it, picks it up again. No dial tone. Rock of ages. I'm on the rock with Uncle D in the sun. The candied apple melts in my fist. The skyline is melting into an ocean of trees above his tree green Tyrolean hat.

His hand snapped to the brim of his hat in a brisk salute as he danced into the hallway that shiny morning to take me out on our longest date. He bowed and kissed Aunt V's gloved hand. She was dressed for the street, in leather. Her boots were laced to the hips. Below the headache band of her beret her face looked horsey and rather sad. The itinerary for the day was in her saddle bag. The Seamen's Institute. The Women's House of Detention. The City Morgue.

Her voice was hoarse from having talked in vain across such distances. She was through with the telephone, its busy signals, bum steers and wrong connections. She'd search for J with the help of our able police, she said, and if necessary J would have to be charged with child desertion, she added in that hoarse voice. Rather would she see J safe behind bars than dangerously on the loose, a drifter in all the waterfront bars if not a floater, eventually.

(A floater, god forbid, Flo says they're dragged by the dozens each day from the river into the morgue, Aunt V remembered.)

She was crushing me in her arms. Her jacket squeaked like a new saddle. Don't hold a grudge against your mother, she warned. Don't let your natural love for your poor mother turn into hate.

Wet kisses on my cheeks and chin. Good girl. Put on something pretty! Hurry. D will look after you. Have fun. Please tuck your tummy in and wear your girdle.

Tummy-tucker mother fucker. Prayers for J's redemption girdle the moon. Aunt V knocks on wood and trots off, leaving the door wide open. Knocks on her saddle bag for double luck, squeezes into her two-seater super sport bucket and vanishes in a smoke screen with a long howl. Blue-bloused pink-cheeked rookie at the corner, suspecting panzered panther attack, draws gun, then drops it back into holster.

Baby-fuzz, says Uncle D with a pink blush. I clasp my belly. In my head or my belly I see mom's sweat shirt striped with the prison bars. Locked up. How will she get away? Aunt V has burned mom's magic supermouse cape. I creep back into the shadow-striped hallway and start to whimper. I plop down on the stairs and hold my belly. I cradle my dummy and sob to break supermom's heart. The entrance door with the eagle creaks shut.

We are going to the zoo, Uncle D says in his clipped city voice. He pretends not to notice my tears. He has turned his back to them and is speaking into the long mirror. I know he can't stand the sight of tears. That's why he loves the monkeys. They don't cry much.

His face is like a monkey's in the mirror, with big eyes older than the hills. Too bad his old friend Jess the chimp won't be in the zoo to greet us. Jess! he calls softly as the ghost of his monkey jumps into the mirror and onto his back, sucking on a mango, clowning.

My anthropoid counterpart behind bars, says Uncle D. He trusted me. There was that wonderful rhythm of habit or repetition as I'd be at his cage the same hour each morning with a dixie cup of café au lait well sweetened to suit his taste while the old guard, an anarchist, would be looking the other way.

Jessie, perched atop the naked make-believe tree of his zoo cage (black tail aloft, black glossy eyes shaded by glossy fingers) is watching for Uncle D, the flash of his safari coat in the central park jungle gym jumble. Our backgrounds were alike, says Uncle D. Ancestral memories run deeper than still waters, and the bars between us did not keep us from communicating and shaking hands.

Uncle D taught Jess to drink from a cup and count up to three—a small recompense for the chimpanzee poetry he learned from Jessie. And when exactly did it occur to him that he might liberate Jess from the cage and make him his roommate? Perhaps it was the anarchist guard, a one-time prisoner himself, who planted the idea in his head and slipped him the key.

Slip me your key, Uncle D. Let's break out of prison. But of course he did not even go through with the plan to help Jess break out of his prison, and yes, sometimes as the jungle odors haunt Uncle D's dreams he finds himself locked up inside the cage, with Jessie gone and the anarchist dangling a banana at him through the bars.

A not entirely unpleasant dream, says Uncle D. Oh, it does grieve him that he lacked the courage to go through with the plan, sneak J out of the zoo under the cover of night, and into the highrise co-op apartment house undetected. However, was the plan really as foolproof as the guard had insisted, and what if they had been detected? He could just imagine the headlines back home in Georgia: HEIR TO HONEYMOON HOTEL ELOPES WITH APE. It might have meant financial ruin, not to speak of the terrible embarrassment to his mother. So, to forestall any gossip or bad publicity for the hotel (and wasn't the anarchist guard already in jail again for having attempted to bomb the AMERICANA) he, D, went south in time to be seen arm in arm with his mother at the official inauguration of the Azalea Queen.

A lovely lunar ceremony on the ante-bellum terrace steps.

But Jess the champ of chimps?

J, says Uncle D, blinking into the mirror, was stolen, kidnapped or abducted from his cage by a party of one or more, still unidentified and supposed to be at large right here in the city.

Uncle D is tipping his hat at himself, I think, as Jessie's ghost has left the mirror. Farewell! He still has that key the guard slipped him, it won't come off the key ring, says

Uncle D, and sometimes, returning home late, he might absently stick the key to Jessie's cage into his own door lock.

Which key is the key to your door, Uncle D?

Get ready, young lady, make yourself pretty! The keys are rattling in his pocket as he pulls away from the mirror and walks outside to wait for me on the stoop in the Sunday sun.

Make yourself pretty to outshine Jess, champ of chimps. I'm jealous of his memory, I brush my hair and dress to kill in clocked blue socks and the white tent dress with the red poppies. No panty girdle, not for me, Aunt V, no underpants. Instead I douse myself with her BONNE NUIT CHERIE and pour the rest of the perfume down the bidet. D Day. Now I am free and light as air. My breasts swing loose, my hair streams bright, my belly weighs less than nothing. Down and out I float into the morning in a blue cloud of good night.

Look: I am irresistible. My breasts swing like two wedding bells under the poppies. We'll swing through the zoo into night. I'm Jessie, feed me a dixie cup of sweet café au lait, feed me a mango. Please rape me on the stoop. No cops in sight. I am your all day all night date for ever. I am your monkey.

But he has thrown the business section of the Times over his face and is sneezing fast and furiously, one sneeze after another like a machine until the stockmarket listings are soaking wet. My allergy, he finally gasps as the fit subsides and he is able to raise his head. But now his spectacles are wet and he sees nothing.

It's the pollution that brought it on, I say half-heartedly, for I'm already suspecting that it's that cursed BONNE NUIT. My tristate transistor states that we've reached the danger level of pollution above and below, I tell him even as he is explaining that the sneezes were brought on by the musk in the scent of which I seem to be using a few drops too many. Musk, says Uncle D, is the glandular animal substance secreted by the male musk deer, muskrat or civet.

Another zoo. And we haven't even moved beyond the nearest vestpocket park. There under the bleary eyes of stumble bum drunks he washes his face at the drinking fountain and swallows a poppy red capsule he has extracted from a snuff box engraved with a B. B stands for Bella, one of his mother's names. A second capsule to be taken in 2 hours, he remembers, staring into the empty snuff box. He forgot to replenish it. At home in his medicine chest he has at least a hundred of those capsules. Ah, well.

Ah, yes, I say, we'll go to your apartment you and me and fill the sneeze box, the love box.

But Uncle D says, thank you, his sinuses have cleared and we'll take a cab to the zoo for a Sunday of fun, though fun time may have to be cut short just a mite, should the sneezing fit reoccur.

My, my! he says, rattling the keys in his pocket. What a pretty dress you have on!

A pretty Sunday funtime dress. The keys in his safari pocket are playing chopsticks. At the drop of a poppy we are out of the vestpocket park and in the crowded green central park rock sea. Uncle D, allergic to noise, is pulling his hat down all the way over his ears as unisex banshees dressed in the stripes and the stars are burning a stack of telephone bills to the beat of transistor drums. They pour the ashes into a coffin. Then they put my dummy with the ashes. From atop a rock a holy rag man is sending black and white balloons on an unmanned moon trip. Pop. The balloons keep bursting above my head. Rock soda pop bottles explode in the trampled grass. A big pig bladder bursts and my dummy is drenched in blood.

Come. This isn't the kind of Sunday fun Aunt V had in mind for you, says Uncle D. He has grabbed me by the elbow and is rushing me off into the African bush. There the sun burns loud through the trees and my poppies burn wet. Pardon me sir, he murmurs, having stepped on the invisible toes of some lady in lover's lane. We sidestep a turd bejeweled with fat, still horseflies. We step aside to let a horseman pass. The round turd shimmers peacock blue. The underbrush smells of Olli. I'm breathing harder.

No, not the chimps, says Uncle D, his hand flipping briefly against my bare arm. It will be years before I dare face them again, though I'm ready for other primates, not dignitaries of the church, you understand, but apes and monkeys—hark! I smell the baboon!

I smell the icecream man. Wonder what makes Aunt V assume that the zoo is clean entertainment. She'd flip her lid if she saw the baboon do his thing. She'd run to phone the hard core anti-porn legion or the sex control bureau in Washington D.C. She'd faint if she saw the baboon swoon come up long and pink in his lanky black fingers to the delighted screams of Sunday kids.

I don't see much. I see a dozen pops, each with his tot aloft on sunday square shoulders, tots licking icecream cones and blowing pink bubble gum into love balloons. Mr. Baboon lets off a fart. I shut my eyes and think of granny-anny's hills, the silver stallion crying for love in the hills as he was growing a fifth leg, fifth pillar of love from his belly down into the poppies.

Buy me a fistful of drumsticks, sticky peanut brittle, candy canes from granny's wagon. Buy me water lilies for my hair.

Water eternal, says Uncle D (we having progressed to the splashing seals) revives the quick but not the dead. The genocide we are committing on the seal folk will surely condemn us to a waterless hell-hole forever. Come!

He is pulling me along with him by the wrist. The Lost & Found Dept. went on strike and we mustn't get separated as we may never be reunited. The park is crawling with tots bawling their lungs out for mommy & daddy. Stay close!

As close as you'll let me, Uncle. My belly throbs. The hippo bellows for his mate. My boobs are aching for you.

Hold me by my sticky hand. Don't lose me. But we have already floated apart in a zoo blue sea of cafeteria umbrellas. It takes some scouting through the mob and food scraps before I spot him as he stands on a chair, frantically flashing the V sign at me across a party of eagle scouts. He is holding the last available table for two. Pulls out a chair for me and bows. Right on. The perfect gentleman from honeymoon lodge.

What may I get you? A dish of no-fat cottage cheese? A slice of melon? Or would you rather have something that sticks to the ribs?

Sticks to the ribs, that's it, buy me a psychedelic ice cream concoction drowned in fudge. Triple portions of hi ho calorie jumbo thrill melts in the mouth 9 different flavors. O no we won't tell Aunt V.

My poppies are glued to the seat of the chair. Uncle D salutes me or a passing West Point cadet and then ducks under fringed umbrellas and gets lost in the chow line. Lost to my eyes. I'm drowsy with the sun and the marine band on my little transistor. The West Point boy is giving me the eye and I nod off from the Halls to the Shores and wake up to the clatter of the tray on which there glows in the plastic goblet a gorgeous ice cream dish through a sunburst of butterscotch sauce (sorry, they're out of fudge).

Uncle D's thumb, girdled by a band aid mildly soiled, dips inadvertently into the sauce as he serves me my ice cream delight. Says he cut his thumb while thumbing through a weighty tome in the rare book section of the Public Library, 42nd St. Branch. Some gilt-edged pages can be razor sharp. Now eat to your heart's dilemma.

That's the one! says a lady to another lady at the next table, pointing at Uncle D with her fork on which is impaled a shrimp as pink as her mouth. The one with the mustache, that's the Armenian or Jew I told you about, the one who was trying to get his hand into my pocketbook at the Public Library on 42nd.

Uncle D is taking a vial of saccharine from his safari pocket to sweeten his lemonade. Never swerves from his diet except every other month when a craving for cheese overwhelms him during the night and makes him devour a pound or so of over-ripe camembert.

The plastic fork with the shrimp is still pointing at him from the next table. Yes, Jay, the Armenian or Jew with the Hitler mustache, no, not that one, the other one, that's the one who was trying to get into my bag . . .

Wipe your mouth, says Uncle D, and let us go.

The maze of blue umbrellas and ice cream boats is tilting away from us, a floating marina. We are on the move again. The lady has swallowed the shrimp, and Uncle D, hands in pockets, doesn't give her a second thought. He is used, he says, to being accused unjustly by older women. He is used to being taken for an Armenian or Hitler. And yes, he vaguely recalls the lady's scratched, wide-open snatch purse, how she had shoved it toward him inch by inch across the long reading table under the ceiling painted with muses and clouds. Heaven knows what may have prompted her tó provoke him. Maybe she was annoyed because of his immersion in Boethius, his Consolation of Philosophy, a sublime opus, executed in a dungeon while B was awaiting his execution in peace, having been condemned to death on four counts.

The freest thoughts, says Uncle D, are born in the shadow of death, in cages or dungeons, and I was drinking deep of B's wisdom when that confounded woman broke the peace and sicked the guard on me. Now it so happened that I was wearing gloves at the time in order not to smudge the rotary photo gravures of B our author at the feet of Lady Philosophy. I'm afraid it was because of the gloves that I had a heck of a time convincing the guard of my innocence in this and related matters.

The fenced-in trees shake with the roar of hungry lions beyond our vision. Uncle D is shaking his head. Once, on the subway platform (Fulton St) a mother tried to have him arrested for exposing himself to her little daughter when actually he never was aware there was a daughter or even a mother. It's odd, he says, that I, a conservative southern reconstructionist should look so criminal to some though I have also been suspected of operating on the other side of the fence, as an FBI agent or Pinkerton man.

Private eyes D jerks down his hat and tip-toes after a priest into the men's room. When he returns his hat is under his arm and the bald spot atop his head lights up like a comic strip bulb. When did you say your aunt expects you home?

I never said. She never did. I know he'd like to know what mom and Aunt V are up to in their black fishnet stockings in the black hourglass night. I know but I won't tell. I don't tell Olli. The sun detours through broken leaves and my lover holds me by the elbow till I feel slender as a laurel tree. He calls me Daphne. Daphne, where to next?

The lions, oh the lions pretty please.

No answer. But one thing is certain: the reptiles, and most especially the snakes are out. He is not ashamed to admit to a horror of snakes, a life-long Phobia on which his sister, little Phoebe, used to play, teasing him, scaring him half to death, cruel child that she was and still is. One summer afternoon she danced ahead of him down the hot beach, dangling a grass snake in front of his nose until he lost all reason and grabbed a piece of driftwood, plank of a shipwrecked boat with the nail sticking out, and started to hit her, nearly putting out one of her eyes with that rusty nail; pursuing her blindly (sic!) back to the hotel grounds where she saved herself from mutilation by diving head-long into the lily pond.

Childhood memoirs of a Southern gent. Did sister Phoebe tell on him? Of course. Did Dad give D a sound whipping?

No, not at all, much worse, daddy ignored him, did not address a single word to him for a whole month. Asked no questions, answered none. Father silence like the grave, with sister Phoebe dancing moon spells around it. Never did put out her snake green eyes. But what if? Guilt, guilt, and every blind man Uncle D encounters becomes his double and he has yet to refuse a blind beggar or fail to send a generous check to The Lighthouse each time they mail him a needle threader. By now he must own hundreds of needle threaders. But there isn't a needle to be found in his house, he suspects.

City pigeons trip over prickly shadows. We are taking another detour through trampled grass. That way we'll never make it in time to watch the wild beasts at their bloody feast, digging into the raw meat, gorging themselves on the government inspected carcass of some old cow. That cow died in Olli's pasture. I'd like to see the feast and yet I don't. I have two minds. And Uncle D would get sick if he watched.

His cheeks, forever waiting to be slapped, are burning with a steady fever. Break that silence, papa, hit your son! But old man river, his or mine, is dead. I wish Aunt V and mom would give each other the silent treatment, but they won't, their fights flood the night, spill over into the sewer, the river, and cross my heart Uncle D, I'd rather not ever go back again to the noise house.

Domestic squabbles are normal enough and you mustn't let them get you down, says Uncle D. Two adults rubbing shoulders under one roof: the very mechanics of such a union spell friction. Noise can't be avoided under the circumstances and the big ears of the little pitcher are bound to hear more than is there. That's why I have, at least so far, preferred to live alone, with no one listening to my solitude, not even Jessie.

The prancing pigeons have taken on the shimmer of peacock feathers, of scoured steel pots. Swirls of rainbows. Let me share your solitude, Uncle D. I'll be your homing pigeon. I've taken off my shoes and socks and my toes curl pink in the grass.

The city fathers, he says, scanning the headlines in the

striped sky, are searching for a final solution to exterminate the pigeons—a sanitary measure, they pretend. Soon we may have to embark for Venice to see a live pigeon.

But Venice, a one-time haven for honeymooners, is rapidly sinking into the ground, so Uncle D or my little transistor informs me. San Marco doomed. The singing Campanile sighs and sinks. The squirrel scampers off, the pigeons vanish as the good humor man, B's best friend, comes tinkling out of the green bush. When I was still little (but already very fat) I used to gobble up his stuff by the dozen, stick, paper and all.

The popsickle & icicle
eloped on a red tricycle

Lipstick-red raspberry sherbet all over my face. Already I am feeling ten pounds younger. You must have been a darling baby boy.

I was, he says, excepting fits of tiger tantrums, a reasonably well adjusted tyke. I honored papa, loved mama, and if sister Phoebe got under my skin it was because she always threatened to drag me off with her on a blind date. We were a well assimilated family in the magnolias, respected by both gentile and colored folks. I was suckled and weaned at the ample breast of pitch-black Penelope. Shut your eyes and suck the fruit. What we don't see don't hurt. I was a blind reader.

Scrawny little D in knee-length breeches got lost in the slave quarters one breathless almond-sweet late afternoon ante bellum. Penny was washing herself in the wooden tub, a black stark naked dream. Get out of here, you little devil! she yelled through the steam and pitched a cake of soap at him. He ran like the devil. The silken twilight was a honeymoon blanket tufted with almond tree blossoms. But he thought he was going blind with the soap in his eyes.

Yes, I say yes, I think of mom, fish-tailed, a dripping dream in the mermaid tub. Oh yes, I take his hand out of his pocket and hold it to my lips, it's soft and smooth like wet rubber, I kiss it (the almond soap smell!) and with my chin I guide his hand to touch my breast under the poppy dress.

I'm sorry! He jumps away from me as though stung by a bee. There is no bee under my poppied bodice. He flexes his arm and the dial of his shockproof wrist watch flashes green. Just when exactly does your mother expect you home, my dear girl?

Never. She's disappeared again, don't you remember? She split and Aunt V will be hunting for her through the night, with the police in tow. Every precinct has been alerted. May we have her photo, ma'm? But none exists. Aunt V snapped her once on the sly in the tumbleweeds, but mom smashed the camera. If you must have a likeness, sir, look for it in the mirror. However, a brief description should help: 5'6". White skin tanned brown, brown hair died blond, eyes nondescript. J jeans, T shirt, Q sneakers. No hat. No purse. Walks with a slouch. Almond-shaped mole on left buttock. Thank you for your patience, officer. The drinks are on me.

I'd rather spend the night in the zoo than go back to the screaming house on the stinking alley. I won't be missed. Mom's on the missing persons list. Besides, I've got my dummy tucked away in my bed, with the radio playing an eagle scout program under the crazy quilt. They can have my dummy. So don't you leave me, daddy-o, if you do I'll throw myself to the lions, I swear. I'm crazy for you.

Crazy. He studies me through thick-lensed glasses, a mustached Christ in a safari coat. Growing pains, he says.

Or puppy love. I don't quite hear him. I am thunderstruck by the sudden apparition of one lioness. For having taken another detour we have made a short cut and find ourselves with the beasts he had hoped to avoid.

But feeding time is over. The lion has retired to his cave. His queen, her majesty of suns and sands, is lying stretched out on the cement of her cage, digesting, dreaming desert dreams of terraced make-believe cities. No leftover bones on her stone couch. No blood on her whiskers. Uncle D can contemplate her through the bars without nausea. She's carved from yellow sandstone. A quiver (dream of bloody meat?) runs through her rib cage and mine. Eat me. I wish I could shrink like A in WL, squeeze through the bars into the cage and put my head with hers on the huge paws and sleep.

May I stay overnight at your place?

I should have added please. Aunt V says never hesitate to ask favors as long as you observe the civil code of general amenities laid down in ETIQUETTE FOR TINY SCREAMERS, rev. ed. Curtsying should be revived as a sign of respect as there is nothing prettier, she says, than the blush of little girl lost dropping a curtsy with the appropriate no sir, and yes madam do. Uncle D's exquisite manners should teach mom and me a lesson. No cuss words from his lips. His cultured speech allows you to ignore some of his less desirable habits, such as keeping his hands in his pockets or picking his nose. He did it when he appeared at her office to inquire about some tenement up for sale on Lex and 111th. Forgive me, madam, may I take up a minute or two of your valuable time?

What charm. Only the deal fell through because the tenement caved in before they got there to look it over. No casualties worth mentioning. A minor disaster, sir. Junkies and junk. I doubt the neighborhood would be your cup of tea. May I drop you some place?

V&D taking tea in the lamplight twilight parlor an hour or so before feeding time. He in big daddy's chair, legs crossed, one hand in his pocket. She reclining à la Récamier on the chaiselongue bleu in her bell flower blue bell-bottom lounging pj's. What big strong hands you have, madam! His eyes under glass were swimming into the froth of her ruffled cuff. Those hands, monsieur, have labored hard for bread! You'd have thought they had marriage in mind, the way they faced each other across the painted porcelain dish of sugared almonds, conversing on mutual comfort, southern funds, the generation gap. What fun it would be, said Aunt V, if our B were a deb, come out with the rest of the lovely young flowers, I watched them in New Orleans, they were presented to society, I watched from the gallery, their bare shoulders, the cleavage as they curtsied all the way down to the floor in genuine dacron. Of course our B wouldn't quite make it, too heavy, besides her mother lacks what it takes to make the social redge. It's no picnic, I swear, those girls have to go through umpty FBI screenings and dress rehearsals for one big curtsy. It is quite a trick to get back on your feet again once you are all the way down.

Down on Bourbon St. with the rest of the strippers, said mom, appearing fresh out of the shower, hair wringing wet, old greasy bathrobe hanging open. Her body in the mirror lion yellow, smooth like rubbed stone. Excuse me, madam, she minced, breaking wind. I didn't know you had the colonel visiting. Don't let me interrupt you, ladies.

Please, Uncle D, keep me, don't leave me, colonel! I bend one knee under the poppies though not enough for him to see. I roll my eyes and fold my hands. Genuflect. Should I tell him of my southern blood? Granny-anny came from southern Croatia. Down she'd go on her knees in front of the altar, the silver ikons black with time. Black mother and child in the altar cage. No father present.

Daddy butchered, cooked and eaten. Will they make soup of my bones?

I can't, he says, shaking his head at the lioness, entertain you in my bachelor quarters unchaperoned. Your aunt would not consider it proper and she is absolutely right.

None of her g.d. business, I'm 13, give a little take a little, bursting with life inside out!

But he says I don't understand, that's just the point and Aunt V is not the only stumbling block. For there is his doorman.

The d-man, what's he got to do with it?

Everything, says Uncle D. He is my conscience, please don't ask why. It must be an obsession as I hardly know the fellow except from sight. He's never said a word to me. He merely opens the plate glass door, tall and accusing in his uniform up to the cleft chin, silent authority, the mere suggestion of his Roman eyes, unblinking under the vizor, cows me and more than once have I sneaked in behind his back to escape detection while he was busy at the curb with one of our co-op wheelchair cases or poodles. One night he caught me in the act. I'll never forget his accusing eyes in the shadow of the vizor in the wall to wall hall mirror. I felt like a thief on my own premises, so abjectly guilty I apologized and slipped him a 10. 10 days it took me before I dared leave my co-op and face him again.

Please ten times please equals love. I won't stay more than 10 minutes, cross my poppies. Am not cowed by your D man. Shall tell him you are my dad.

But the answer still zero. O no. No guest has entered his apartment for he could not endure the sense of loss once the visitor has departed again to leave him with nothing except himself and his library alphabetically arranged up to the ceiling.

What's hanging from your ceiling, Uncle D? The lioness woke up and stared at nothing through mom's glazed, yellow eyes. But we had already left her behind and the zoo was a memory. Uncle D had stretched out in the grass, with the hat over his face. Was he asleep? Gray boulders, ice age travelers streaked glazier green were grazing about him. I was standing on the highest rock in a strong wind. It blew up my tent dress. I pulled it down and clamped it fast between my knees. I was bigger than the city, the windy skyscrapers moon sail cloud rakers that were surging over the horizon of rocks or trees. Highrise co-op billion dollar thrills with terraces exclusive for suicides. Pay off or jump! Families on the move to the suburbs at an astronomic rate bumper to bumper, my transistor announcer mumbles through rocky nights. Widows, senators, jockeys and junkies are feeling the pinch of the slump. Down all the way. Tighten your seat belts. Those who failed to pack and leave be seated please. Children, wheelchair commuters and basket cases will be given separate but equal facilities. No defecating in the bunker. Standard oil has donated dog bars and musical toilets to be used at your own risk. Remember your blind doorman.

Fun program. Radio-active dialogue. Dial our number any time. Listener participation raises public interest and lowers production costs. Go to it, boys and girls. The number is. Zero.

The sun is. I couldn't tell one highrise co-op from another, they all were rushing past too fast, stampeding down the windy horizon. I couldn't spot the cathedral where my old dentist drills across the hall at a right angle from Aunt V's old therapist, she spitting up her bloody past on the vinyl couch while I'd be spitting out my last bloody milk tooth. Sweet tooth has cavities galore. Waiting for mom at Rumpelmayer's, Rumpelstiltskin threw up 10 petits fours in the Marie Antoinette toilette to a Mozart minuet taped in Salzburg. My inners felt rotten. Use your finger, said Aunt V, holding my head. Shove your finger down your throat. A high-class neighborhood for V girls and Pulitzer poets. Organ music and canned laughter are piped into the stuck elevators to lift the sagging spirits of aging AMA men and Blue Cross agents.

It would take a life-time to fall from my dentist's window into the CP lake among the row boats. He drills in a penthouse. From where I stood, high on the rock, I could not see his house or Uncle D's, much though I searched the clouds. Uncle D was still lying stretched out in the squashed grass and I wondered was he really asleep under the Tyrolean hat with the speckled feather or was he faking so as to catch me red-handed should I decide to climb down and get my hands at his keys. He looked defenseless, flat on his back in the nothing grass amid the rocks of the finished ice age, and anyone might steal his keys. The tall boy with the vizored cap might do it. He had jumped out of the bushes and was snapping my picture from below with an Instamatic. Gotcha, cutie. How about you and me going rowing down the lake a piece like a quick dream?

I dropped off the rock and into his bulging arms. All muscle, feel, he said. Squeeze as hard as you can. Biceps like solid rock. How about that! I said my daddy was asleep. We were running across the meadow, chasing a pigeon. He looked like Olli. I called him O for old times sake. He called me Chubby. He said he was a QDS messenger boy. Q stands for quick. He said, in my line of work you meet all kinds. No, Chubby, we don't need your daddy's keys. A boat is all we need for 10 sweet minutes.

Seems everybody I know wants to deliver quick. His hands were sweating in my arm pits, I didn't say stop. The lake was overflowing with lopsided boats packed with screaming babies and picnic hampers. Two guys kept ramming each other. They lost their oars. I couldn't see the water for the garbage. My QDS messenger boy rowed like a pro smack into another boat. A mother lunged out and hit him over the head with a Spanish guitar.

There's too many people, he said, too many spades and spics on the fucking lake, too much garbage, he said, tossing out a cup cake wrapper. Here, have a bite. I took a big bite off the top. Stole all the pink icing. He turned up the transistor loud for mood tunes. The cup cake slipped out of my mouth and under my seat. Sit still, Chubby. We'll pick it up later.

I said it was soggy, deliver, the bottom of the boat was slimy green. Sit still, he said. His head was under my poppy dress. I screamed and rocked the boat. I made it capsize. I dumped myself plump into the lake. Ophelia afloat in the garbage. I swallowed a tadpole. The lake patrol fished me out.

You shouldn't have rocked the boat, miss. Shouldn't row solo, ain't safe. Next time take your boy friend.

Poppy dress clinging, dripping, I scooted back across the meadow through flying saucers. My hair was dripping like mom's after the shower. My shoe got stuck in a pot hole. I caught a frisbee. Uncle D didn't see me. He was circling the rock, and by the way he kept turning his head to the left and the right, a child would have known that he was worried out of his head over me.

Here I am, Uncle D, soaked to the skin. Was raped by a QDS messenger boy in a capsized canoe while you were asleep.

Uncle D bent down and picked up a stick and beat it against his thigh as he looked at me dark and enraged from under the brim of his hat without a single word of either reproach or relief.

He was letting me have it, not even touching me, just being silent like his dad while the rock cast the longest shadow. My teeth were chattering in the cold wind. But he said nothing. I said, Aunt V will blow her lid when I come home one soggy, filthy mess. You were supposed to keep an eye on me, but how could you, Uncle D, you were out cold. It's not your fault and I'll make up a story so she won't blame you.

He whipped the stick through the air with such anger it whistled. I heard the whistle and the smack as it came down on his thigh. He still was giving me the silent treatment, but he was raging in his head. His face was beautiful with rage and the veins on his temples were swollen and blue like granny-anny's. I thought how beautiful he was and how the rock might be a house for two, with a ledge like a terrace and on it a pop bottle with a single blue flower growing from it all alone. O daddy, my teeth were chattering to scare the wind. Honest, I'm sorry, dad, I didn't mean to, not your fault if I catch pneumonia. I'll tell Aunt V I fell into a sewer hole while a priest was blessing your cross.

I coughed to move the rock. He tossed me his coat. I tossed it back at him—Thanks! Just lend me cab fare, Aunt V must be having a fit, two persons missing, mom and me.

What if the QDS messenger boy knocked me up? But that's my problem.

The look he gave me across the terrace, the flower! I was coughing my lungs out and again he tossed me his coat, this time to land right on my head. The stick broke on his thigh. He broke the silence. Put on that coat, you little monster! If I were half a man I'd wash my hands of you and make you walk home. Barefoot!

Push the buttons and go station hopping through the night. Blues, jazz & rock. News by the clock. VATICAN URGES BAN OF SPERM PRODUCING DOLLS FOR GROUPIES. NOW BACK TO THE MARATHON TALK FEST. DIAL RADIO DIALOGUE FOR A SHOULDER TO CRY ON. SORRY. THE SWITCHBOARD'S BLOWN UP.

I wouldn't dream of phoning for that shoulder, I switch to statistics. Did he say it's in Chile or China that a new baby is born every five seconds? Inhale, count up to five, relax and PRONTO. Trigger your own population explosion. Maybe I ought to start getting into some of Aunt V's baby care books. She has a whole library of do-it-yourself manuals, CREATIVE ASPECTS OF BREAST FEEDING and HOW TO MAKE THE BEST OF YOUR MENOPAUSE. THE FATHER ROLE OF THE AMERICAN MOTHER had a chapter ripped out. I think mom did it. I wonder what the chapter said and why she ripped it out long before I was born.

Roll over in bed in the rain. I feel like a lopsided whale with Jonah inside me, or maybe it is Joanna? They're silent in the talking room below. Mom has come back to us alive out of her own strange whale. Will they give a fancy dress ball to celebrate her return from the bottom of the roaring sea? Will Uncle D come to the ball disguised as his doorman? I have not seen him again, not since that broken Sunday when he stopped a cab and, tightlipped, directed me to sit in the back alone while he got into the front with the driver who had the ball game going full blast. Each time Uncle D reached out to lower the volume the cabbie turned it up until the noise was too much even for me. I was shivering under the safari coat and my face in the rear mirror was like a jellyfish, with the hair stringy like old weeds. No shoulder for me to cry on except my own. The last whiff of BONNE NUIT CHERIE had drowned in the lake and I felt like a dead fish. But then the mirror flashed crimson. The sun showed huge on the river horizon and the sailors on deck of the destroyer Wisconsin were sliding like black cut-outs across the disk of that unreal sun.

I hope you have your key! Uncle D warned through the ballgame. The cabbie had swung into our alley and the V house appeared deserted for ever, with the windows shuttered and dried dog piss zigzagging down the stoop. I climbed the stoop and pretended to reach for the key under the ruined poppies. Uncle D had moved to the back seat which some anonymous hood had slashed with a knife. He fingered the damp coat I had left for him neatly folded, but he did not put it on and in a moment he had cranked up the window to show that we had split for good. Goodbye. His eyes were trained on me like two gun barrels even as the cab was already moving again, and I knew then without a doubt that I had lost my chance to get past his doorman. Off-limits for me the gorgeous co-op with its Turkish divans and royal blue baths. Not for me the almond sweet soap in the silver shell, the crested towels, the heavy shower curtain with his jockstrap hung up to dry and drip drop rain into my mouth, no, I would never get to pop popcorn, toast marshmallows over his fire or touch his dad's cartridged silver cigar case. All that was finished, had drowned in the lake with my key.

Goodbye, a soda bottle explodes in the backyard, tossed over the wall by a stranger. I doubt that anyone will be at home. The house is too silent. Aunt V must still be chasing after mom through all the boroughs. So what, I don't mind flopping down in the dog piss and waiting for somebody to make it home and let me in. A burglar would do. Why not? I'd help him rob her for all she is worth which is plenty, I'll help him find the hole behind the Spanish tile where she keeps her sterling golf coast cup and phony bracelets. The real ones are in the bank vault and the opal is gone anyway, was cracked, I forgot against the dashboard of whose car, in the High Atlas.

Opaline fire, a stick up, why not, just let me keep my little transistor, mister, I'll give you a guided tour through the house free. But maybe the thieves are already at work inside, I hear odd noises, and before I have time to knock on wood with the american eagle the door opens, first to a crack, then wide as the world and there is Aunt V dressed to her chin in her Saigon pj's or whatever else it is she's wearing with Peace on it. She's back! She's back! she cries, sweeping me up in her arms and planting a kiss on top of my head, it makes me feel like Miss Universe being crowned though I already have a notion that it isn't me she's welcoming back—in fact I doubt she quite realizes I've been away—no, no it isn't my return she's celebrating. It's mom who has come back to us, I know. And now I begin to tremble, not as from cold but from the inside out until I am floating even as Aunt V is holding me fast against her initialed bosom

(VJVJ)—she's back! she's back!—now the whole world is my lover, I don't even mind Aunt V, I almost like her smell of Edelweiss lotion and sherry and camembert, I'm happy she isn't asking me what kind of a day I had in the zoo or why I look such a fright.

Mom's back!

Hush, baby, we don't want to wake her up! Aunt V seals her pursed lips with her index finger. The shade of her nail polish—scorched earth number 5—matches her lipstick. Hush! I hear mom snore familiar snores under a night umbrella of twitching stars. Black tapers burn white on the dining table, its hastily abandoned snack à deux. Rose petals swim in the silver terrine in the borscht, and a roach in the espresso cup. On the bear rug an empty matchbook and on the mantle mom's pipe. And draped across the Chinese vase her tattered old bathrobe stained with last month's menstrual blood in the mirror.

Oh yes, you're back all right. Sleep tight. Good night.

Back? No, not quite, not really. It would take a while before she'd turn up in reality, the real mom or J. The one who was snoring my life away in the big bed upstairs, well, you might call her a stand-in or substitute mom. I wouldn't call her an impostor. She had not asked for the part. She simply had been taken in by Aunt V and given a new identity for the duration.

When she came creeping downstairs the morning after, in mom's bathrobe and with an ice bag tied to her head I did not for a moment doubt that she was mom. Good morning, I said, pretending she never had been away, and keeping my voice down so as not to make her head worse. Me and Uncle D, we had a ball at the zoo.

She stared at me blank through the eye slits of a white beauty mask. And though I'd never known mom to do anything with her face except to wash it occasionally, it yet did not dawn on me that what I saw creep down the stairs was not my real mom. Just wait till I tell you about Uncle D's super deluxe love duplex, I said as softly as I could in my excitement. You guessed right, mom. The man is sick.

She was clutching the banister for support, her eyeballs rolling in the slits of the mask. Then she gulped and said, hey, kid, I'm sick myself. Do they have a second john in this joint? The one upstairs don't flush.

Now, the question alone might have been a give-away if mom hadn't asked that very same question herself, often in the middle of night. So I said, easy, mom. And I told her to lean on me as I helped her down the rest of the steps and to one of our innumerable antiqued toilets.

But I guess it was really a game from the start for all of us. We had been worn out waiting for mom, and to make believe that this J2 was J broke the tension like a downpour after a long dry spell. For a while we were happier than we had been for years. Everybody got into the act, even Flo, and J2 played her part like an old trooper, unless of course she was too tanked or spaced out.

She may have been both on that crazy Sunday when Aunt V had discovered her through the window guards of a run-down waterfront saloon in Brooklyn, one borough of many where she had been chasing after mom in a patrol car with two friendly cops from the homicide squad, or the bomb squad, she had forgotten which.

A nerve-shattering ride. I saw you raped, murdered and maimed inside an army locker, Aunt V might say to the real or the false J as she would go over the minutes of that cruel day. She thought she was losing her head, literally, what with her personal anguish and crime reports getting all scrambled up inside the patrol car, its never-ending emergency messages over the speaker—A STIFF IN Q PARK * TWO FLOATERS IN B BAY * PROCEED TO INTERSECTION V&J * ALLEGED CHILD MOLESTER D HIDING IN AQUARIUM—darling, such terrible goings-on, crimes committed by lovers and leftists all over the city, I was ready to jump off W Bridge.

Hang on, lady. If you try to jump we'll have to book you. We'll find the girl for you dead or alive. Who is she—your niece?

My niece and minor dependent. Oh those angelic guardians of the law.

Hang on, tried my darndest, had come to the end of my rope or pretty near it when we happened to pass this shady no-good saloon . . . .

STOP, OFFICER!

J2 as spied by Aunt V and identified through the lozenge of the window guard: Ample torso slumped half-way over the bar. Voluptuous rump touching the edge of the barstool. Must have gained pounds and pounds. But unchanged otherwise. Same slouch or slump. Same hair palegold rheingold dripping down from under the green beret. Ends of moist hair like crushed tulips.

Right on the button, officers! That's my niece, the green beret in the sequined turtleneck and combat boots. Grab her before she escapes through the kitchen. You won't regret it.

Sure won't. That's what we're here for, lady.

Aunt V, lowering her eyes so as not to witness possible bloodshed, was biding her time by the fire hydrant while the two commandos marched inside and past a crap game straight after the niece who was about to give them the slip through the back door when they stopped her in her tracks and ordered her to return to her aunt or else.

Else what? Book her for prostitution or for impersonating a green beret? No matter. Mission accomplished.

Some scene it must have been, that reunion between two sisters who never had laid eyes on each other before. (A page out of Ripley's BELIEVE IT OR NOT she admitted much later.) She hugged and kissed J2, she forgave her for all past sins and extracted from her a solemn oath of 100% fidelity from here on and forevermore unto the grave.

My new mother may have been puzzled to find herself forgiven by a complete stranger and welcomed back to a house she never had occupied. But weirder things had happened to her and she figured that perhaps the fuzz, tired of hauling her in again on the same old charges, had passed her on into the custody of the salvation army. However, she heard no hymns, no horns or drums. The cops had discreetly vanished and the only uniform she saw was that of a legless soldier who was propelling himself on a dolly fast into space.

Fast faster o my J bird! Aunt V exclaimed. J2 who was under the weather misunderstood. She thought the lady in genuine leather had called her a jail bird. The street seemed out of focus and everything happened so fast or so slow, she couldn't keep track. The cripple, his olive drab torso, had disappeared. Yet the whir of his dolly continued wild in her ears and she wasn't sure if she herself was not the cripple wheeling herself downgrade and into space.

She got sick and passed out at the curb and when she came to she was lying on the floor of a strange house.

So there was my new mom, solid and big-boned, quite a few years older than my old mom, I guess, and certainly bigger. Mom's tight jeans couldn't possibly fit her and Aunt V had to buy a larger pair which she first bleached, stained, ripped, frazzled and kicked about the basement for that genuine J look before she thought them right for wear. And my new mom was quite willing to follow suggestions as long as they did not seem unreasonable, such as her switching to gin when she had been a whiskey boozer all her life. But she was perfectly agreeable to rinsing out her mouth with mom's gin before bedtime to smell the part, and to puff on mom's short pipe, and slop about the house barefoot without make-up or scent. Soon, if you saw her in the mirror as she would slouch and weave her way through another day, you could not tell her apart from mom. And yet Aunt V felt from the beginning that something was missing, that some quality had gotten lost—what was it? Ah yes, the house had become so quiet. There was no foul language, no smashing of glasses and mirrors, no deathly threats in the night. My new mom talked and talked, it's true, but she talked softly, she never raised her voice or a hand.

Hit me! Aunt V's scream would travel the night waves— in vain. J2 said she wouldn't dream of hurting her gracious hostess. It wasn't, she said, her bag, and would V please stop screaming as the neighbors might wake up and call the cops.

No one can hear us! Aunt V would wail through the night. The house next door is boarded up and the cops are my pals. Please J rough me up knock me out . . . .

But my new mom stood firm. Uh-uh. No dice. I'm keeping my nose clean.

Yes, for a while we lived a serene, normal life. At bedtime she would bring her bottle to my room and tuck me in and tell me a story—the story of her life, she said, though each time she had a different version. She was raised in a convent, she was sold into child prostitution. She was divorced, she never had married, she was the widow of an admiral and the daughter of a Sardinian sadist or sadistic sardine. Each night she put on a different tape for me. We really related.

Strange, as she'd turn the lamp shade to have the light shine on the ceiling I'd feel as though it was actually mom's shadow I'd see move like a bear across the wall. And though I could count on the fingers of half a hand the number of times mom had stumbled into my room (by mere accident) the feeling would yet persist, soft and heavy. Cliff-hanging at the edge of a dream I'd take hold of her big hand and put it under my cheek on the pillow for company as her voice would hum on like a non-stop transistor talk show, down into sleep.

She was a talk show all by herself, and I began to ask myself if she mightn't be my real mother. I loved her stories—all those pasts, parents and partners she'd had— and I was truly sad to see her go and hear Aunt V call her a compulsive gabber and liar whose name didn't even start with a J.

I was old enough to be told, Aunt V said, sniffing a little, that the creature who had posed as my mother was nothing more than a cheap prostitute. Those whores were all alike, stealing, drinking or shooting up so as to numb their senses against intercourse by the clock or similar filth. And how was the American home to survive against such odds? she demanded, blowing her nose as she looked mournfully down at the unkempt bear rug.

No mom of any kind in the house to sleep it off on that rug. J2 had been sent packing during a stormy scene: Aunt

V had discovered that the money J2 had wheedled out of her to support a crippled brother had gone to support a pimp—no cripple he! Aunt V had put a tail on them and traced the pair from an apartment house in Brooklyn Heights to downtown Manhattan and BANGS.

Out! Out! And don't you ever show your face in my house again! Don't you dare give my phone number to your pimp!

J2's reply to Aunt V's outburst was so forceful it would have made mom blush. A bicycle chain of unexpected four letter words came beating down on Aunt V, familiarly, and the pitch of J2's voice was all at once so like J's, Aunt V was about to forgive and forget. Too late. The front door slammed shut with such force one of the wall mirrors fell and broke on the tiles as though flung there by J's hand, Aunt V whispered, shuddering. J2's profanities continued to ring from the alley. And Aunt V, peering through the louver slats into the sunny gutter whispered helplessly, oh my dear god, she stomps just like your ma.

So she was banished and I missed her company more than I would have expected. Even the oatmeal and egg white she'd slap on her face to iron out those laughing lines and premature wrinkles, she'd say, now seemed delicious to me though at the time they almost ruined my appetite. She'd boil or whip up a beauty mask for herself while Aunt V would be at the office, making a fortune. And Flo who wouldn't have let my old mom come near the kitchen, simply ignored my new mom.

J2's eyes, small, spotted and bright, would shine like lady bugs through the mask as she would ask me to turn the transistor up to shut her up for if she went on gabbing the way she always did a mile a minute the mask might drop off

and good food would be wasted on nothing when half the
world was going hungry though billions of tons of food, she
said, were being dumped into the ocean for reasons of a
sound economy, she had read in the News.

There I go gabbing again. Why don't you shut me up,
kid!

I tried to, I tuned in on Teenager's Hygiene Hour—
STAMP OUT VD SMACK SOCK IT TO THEM WITH A
PRAYER NEVER FORGET TO REMIND YOUR DATE
THAT VD IS AMERICA'S CHILD KILLER NUMBER
ONE—when she'd be off rapping, bits of oatmeal dropping
down her blouse as she'd nod and say, it's true, kid, take it
from the horse's mouth, carry your own supply of good
quality rubbers. Don't leave it to the boys, kid. Come prepared. And she'd follow up with a long warning list of VD
symptoms and how some babies were born blind. Then she
might cry a little and the mask would fall to pieces gray and
sad.

Oh yes, I liked her. She treated me like an equal, unlike
Aunt V who thought I was still a virgin at 13 when I had
started so long ago—was it with the window washer at ten? I
can't remember.

Sometimes I almost wanted to tell her about my being
pregnant, but I always caught myself in time as I could
never be sure she mightn't let Aunt V in on my sècret. She
wouldn't have done it purposely, no, but there was no
telling how much she might spill once she hit the bottle hard
enough or was on speed.

At such times nothing could switch her off as she would
talk without a pause about aṇything that might or mightn't
have happened. Yes, even when she was alone or imagined
herself alone she'd keep at it. I think that's how Aunt V
learned about the pimp and those money transactions: my

new mom must have had a lover's quarrel with him in her head in the talking room or in bed in her sleep.

The wet sky gurgles in the drain pipes. Breathe deep, breathe low. Aunt V is the last one I'd want to get wind of my secret. She would never let me have my baby. She'd drag me to her specialist so fast it won't be funny and have me first in line for a penthouse abortion de luxe with a view on Lincoln Center.

A package deal. Abortion fee includes six ballet lessons. Stretched out on my back I hear the guitar strings stretched tight across the wet night sky. Earth preservation interview on my transistor suggests the breeding of mini people. Fantastic! Would you mind enlarging on this, professor? Not at all. Breed them tiny and mother earth will yield enough for everyone.

Stand small, not tall. I feel ant-sized people crawl all over mother earth or me, their tiny feet tripping across my sleep. Mini people & mini mass transportation. Rush hour in the old ant hill. One skyscraper, say the empire state, could house billions. Sounds scary? Don't panic. Think! Roll up your mini sleeves and dig those ditches. One tenth of an inch of rain may spell your extinction. But first a word from our weatherman in central park: The forecast is rain, not snow.

But I can see them on my window pane, small crystal stars forming, dissolving. When it's time for my baby to come out and become a statistic, it will be winter. How long ago the hills and Olli seem, like tiny specks of snow on snow-white paper. If I told him for sure I got his loaf in my oven, would he start filching cigars from under his dad's counter to hand out to his class mates on B day? But no, he'd cut me dead if I told him he knocked me up whether he did or not he likes nice girls and he'd be the last one I'd tell for he would never do as the father I have in mind. I prefer a man with class.

Wolves make tender, reliable fathers, said Uncle D in the zoo, and, yes, I could pretend for laughs that he was the human wolf. How that would make him run like a demon back to his honeymoon island, his mother's womb-tomb. No, Uncle D, stay where you are, you are safe. If I must choose a father for me and my child I may yet choose a real wolf.

But no, the baby is mine alone and I want to keep it that way as long as I can. I'll hold on to my secret. Thank god I'm fat. Nothing will show. No one will know which part of me is really only me. We're one and sometimes I almost wish we could stay like that forever, me and her and him, all three of us in one. I hope it's twins.

Or triplets? But not a litter like that poor woman had on my transistor, her babies were like tiny naked rats, all of them died, fertility pills, they can kill you, I wouldn't let those doctors kill me, whatever they prescribe I flush down the toilet fast. She's gained again! they cry. God, are they dumb! They haven't the faintest notion what makes my breasts swell. My nipples feel sticky and tender. They stiffen at the merest touch. I'll breastfeed you as long as you like, you bet your sweet life, my child.

Maybe I'd rather share my secret with somebody after all? The night before the great bust when my new mom was to be given her walking papers, I pressed her big hand to my belly and asked did she feel something kick. But she didn't react one way or another. I think she was already suspecting that Aunt V had found her out and she was busy in her head trying to cover up for her pimp and herself though of course it was too late for that and the following day she was banished.

I still can hear it, the sudden bang of the door, the crash of the mirror. I looked at myself in the shards that were scattered across the tiles, and saw my face cut up into jagged pieces as though with a razor.

Put on your shoes! You'll step into glass! warned Aunt V. She was wearing green rubber gloves. Squatting on her heels she picked up the mirror shards, looking at her face in each of them before she dropped them one by one slowly into an old flower pot.

Finished our interlude of peace. J2 is but a memory and the hunt for mom is being resumed with new vigor. Now the phones downstairs, upstairs or under the stairs are jingling again, are buzzing with rumors, false clues, commiserations from well-meaning sisters as well as queries from bewildered strangers who call in answer to an ad Aunt V has put into the wall street journal. The ad has appeared as specified, in fat print, but with most of the words so distorted it's obvious, she says, that one of her enemies (Q?) is out to make her the laughing stock of the underground sorority.

ANNI ONE WITH POSITIVE CLAWS AS TO J'S WHIRABOOTS PLEASE TO COONTACT V'S DEMON ***CRASH REWARD FLESH***

Etcetera. Significantly, our telephone number has been printed without an error. And so we are being swamped with calls, some of them so obscene Aunt V has passed them on to the FBI for decoding. And I have been strictly forbidden to answer the phone after dark. For it is under the cover of night, she warns me, that perverts and pollsters crawl into those anonymous phone booths reeking with stale cigar smoke and semen. Of course most city pay phones are out of order, having been jammed, kicked in, ripped off and out, she remembers, if they haven't already been sealed off by ma bell to forestall vandalism. But a pervert never is at a loss to find a pay phone which still functions, and no, she can't afford to ignore the calls. She must answer each, must listen closely to every foul proposition, every four letter word, as there is always a chance that within the flood of obscenities she might detect one hint as to J's whereabouts.

So she endures and follows up. J has been observed at BANGS, working the late late shift as a topless waitress? Aunt V must look into it, must join the eyeless plaster statues at the wee hours in a smell of vaginal sprays, beer, vomit and torn velvet hangings. Huge-assed waitresses sail through the smoke. Not a J in the whole lot. Bare chests athletic. No hair. Little mother, play me that Volga song again on your bazooka. Shake 'em and I'll buy you another bullshot. J who? Haven't seen her in ages. Q's going straight with a research professor in Saudi Arabia. T who? My god, this bar is starting to cave in again. Hold me tight, don't split, mother . . .

I must have been ten that winter when I was huddling under the stairs with the window washer. We kissed. The foghorn was blasting away through the ice on the river. I lied about my age. Fifteen, I said. Across the hall the talking room windows flapped open and shut and snow fell into his bucket under the ladder. I said, please do it to me, Mr. Window Washer, I give it away to you. But he said, no thanks, it's too risky. You're just a baby. Where's your mom?

Lost in the snow, oh Mr. Window Washer pretty please. We are alone in the big house. We kissed. His mustache tickled my nose. I sneezed and spread myself out for him on the floor by the deacon's chest under the stairs. But he said, cut it out, jail bait, I don't take no chances with little kids. Where's your mom?

The foghorn sounded sadder than the night. I started to bawl, I said, I know what's with you, mister, you are a homofairifag, that's what's with you. Then the foghorn bellowed, he grabbed me by the throat—fat little whore! I'll learn you!—the bucket rattled in the talking room. The windows flew shut. His dick was huge, it nearly split me in two. That night when Aunt V came home from another mom hunt she saw the blood stains on my pants and said, you can't be menstruating yet? You're just a baby.

The slimy blood, the pain, perhaps that's how it will be when the baby tears loose. Sometimes I can feel it tear through my sleep, the pain of that winter day, though I can't remember much when I wake up. Not even when I am sitting under the stairs on the deacon's chest do I remember. Three years is a life time. And Aunt V has had the wooden floor in the hallway covered with moorish tiles in blue and yellow on white. No red. The slanting hall mirror reflects the geometric pattern of a mosque or a harem.

Did mom leave snow tracks when she returned alone by herself that winter, coatless and frozen? It never would be Aunt V who'd find her and bring her back home. Mom always would come back in the end by herself. Where else could she go, in the end? She'd creep into the house through the back door, drained, sallow and shrunken so that she would seem to me like a starved runaway child or a fugitive dog that's been betrayed and beaten once too often by its own master.

Each time mom returned I had this feeling that she was the victim of some secret persecution beyond my understanding. Yet wasn't it Aunt V who called herself the victim? Mom would return meek and chastised, too weak to speak as Aunt V would deliver herself of all that anguish and grief she had stored up during mom's mysterious absence. While mom would sway sideways in an imaginary wind, dull-eyed, not hearing anything maybe and only waiting to go to sleep.

She would sleep and sleep after those trips into the unknown—unknown to us and even to her, it seemed, as she'd have only a blurred memory if any of where she had been, with whom. Aunt V, tortured by jealousy and by the old compulsion to get an itemized account of reality, could not accept mom's vagueness. I implore you, J! Try to remember at least something, start with a face or a place, cough it up, spit it out, I'll forgive you.

And mom would try, might recall through a sleep-tangled frown that at one point (but when!) she woke up (but where!) and there was that brown dog (a doberman pincher?) lying stretched out on the floor alongside the bed, and she in bed with a murderous headache, the dog whining, whining till she thought her brain was exploding inside her head. Yes, she remembered the dog.

Never mind the dog, Aunt V would say in a tremulant voice. Who was in bed with you!

But mom would shake her head and say that she couldn't after all be sure that she hadn't dreamed it. For in the wake of her long absences, fragments of reality, dogs, bottles, men, women, beds, would briefly be washed ashore only to be swallowed up again by another dream wave and she could be sure of nothing except of those murderous headaches the morning after.

J, please! Don't torment me, whose bed were you in!

But mom would shake her head again, puzzled. That whining dog—had she dreamed him up? Had she dreamed it, her hitting him over the head with the whip that had been lying across the bed? And yet she seemed to recall it so clearly, that sudden trickle of blood from one eye and her kneeling down by him and licking away the blood, with the dog not snapping at her and only faintly growling.

I wonder who's his master . . .mom might say.

Who was in your bed! Aunt V might ask again, biting her knuckles. But mom would reveal nothing. Her head would drop back into the pillows and she would sleep.

Then Aunt V might don a starched white smock and decide that she wasn't going to question mom again until mom was fit to be questioned. Your poor mother, she might say to me, must be treated like a patient after a severe, near fatal accident. And she would throw a blanket over mom and lower the lights and make the sign of the cross over mom's head.

She'd lock away mom's pipe, tobacco and gin. And mom, transparent as a shadow (sliding through closed doors and walls, it would seem to me) would be too weak to break into the liquor cabinet. She'd let herself be nursed by Aunt V who'd glide about like a devoted nun in white, feeding vitamins to mom and keeping passion in harness even as she'd soap mom's back in the mermaid tub. And mom would quietly submit to all the rules, eat, sleep, abstain, and drink a quart of fortified milk daily as though she were pregnant with me or my twin all over again.

No arguments from mom during such periods of con-valescence. No smashing of mirrors or wild-eyed cursing, only a weak mumble as she breaks a glass by accident and spills the milk on the bear rug. Each time she returns from the unknown, ghostlike and shaking, we have that interlude of peace like an armistice while Aunt V is coaxing her back to life, forgetting maybe that as soon as mom has been revived the mirrors will come crashing down and insults will fly with the flying glass through the night. Kaput, as the window washer had said to me under the stairs in the snow long ago.

Ghostlike, mom passes through the mirrors as though through a blizzard, staring into each mirror in search of that lost face or moment Aunt V so desperately wants her to catch and nail down. But there is nothing in the mirror to help mom remember and she may not even recognize her own face, may stare into a void, blankly or scared because of that big hole in her memory, and yes, I saw her stare that way at the man who stood in the entrance door in a bitter wind, saying, Janie, won't you ask me in for a drink, don't stare at me like that, Jenny, you can't already have forgotten me, Atlantic City, we swiped a wheelchair and I wheeled you down the boardwalk in the light of the moon, what a gas, Jackie, bloody maries for breakfast in bed, the sheets looked like we'd been through a bloodbath, Josephine, don't you remember daddy? You're too much.

Too much of him, all bulk in that quilted orange hunting vest. Big, swarthy, sweaty. He's no dad of mine. Hair red. Face red like Olli's in cold weather. I saw him lean in the open door as I was coming back from the pier with my fishing line and the keys and condoms I had fished from the river where the wind made whitecaps and the gulls fought, screeching, over the garbage. Don't give me any shit, he said to mom. You broke the bidet and I got stuck with the bill.

Broke what? Mom, staring, blank and lost, tried to remember.

Convention of computer salemen in A.C. Does that ring a bell, Jemima? The weather freezing cold at 2 am and you coming out of the water stark naked jesus the beach patrol had picked up the clothes you'd left in a pile in the sand, they thought those clothes belonged to that kid who'd drowned himself—subversive student from Michigan U. What are you staring at me like that for, Jocasta?

She shut her eyes to his clouded face and tried to get hold of some memory item, a bottle of Smirnoff 100 proof; three old ladies on a bench, chatting; or the A.C. hotel, its concave monster facade glued together from giant turds or seashells with the sea beyond gray, furrowed like the hide of an ancient rhino—yes, she remembered the gray sea, the cracked sand like a jigsaw puzzle with too many pieces missing or lost including herself. She couldn't fit herself into the puzzle, nor him either, and so with a pathetic smile she shook her head and said, sorry, I don't seem to be able to place you.

Not able to place me! His red-knuckled fist (broad like Olli's) was suddenly at her chin as if to hit her. But then he dropped it and laughed out loud, OK Judy, if that's how you want to play it just give me back my sportsmen's belt, steerhide leather, solid silver buckle, gift from the wife, I'd better not come home without it, considering. . . .

Did Aunt V find out about the computer salesman or were there others out of the frozen sea? She may have answered the door for one of those callers, pretending she was mom's big sister, luring him into the talking room and

getting him drunk enough to worm out of him whatever
details she could about torn bedsheets, whining dogs, forni-
cation in oceans of bloody maries. Big sister's features con-
torted into a mask of hilarity. What did you say the name of
that hotel was—THE TROUBADOUR? They have topless
waitresses, don't they?

You bet, topless and bottomless too, haha, another wee
drinkie, why not, madam, we only live once.

Yes, only once. Thank god for that. Charm bracelets,
slave bracelets quiver, the pearl choker around her gulping
throat glistens as though with tears as she forces a smile and
pours her best scotch for the pig. Topless *and* bottomless? I
hope my little sister wasn't embarrassed!

She didn't look that way to me, madam . . . He hums and
haws and downs another double scotch. Smacks, licks his
lips, grins, blinks through guarded eyes. Aunt V has quickly
guessed that he is itching to tell her something dirty, a
locker room story not fit for the ears of a lady though
wouldn't it be fun to see her blush . . .

I suppose my kid sister had a go with one of the waitresses?

Holy mackerel, madam, how did you guess!

(Wish I could gouge out his dirty-blue eyes, tear his pig
snout to shreds with my long fingernails, may god strike
him dead, but not right away, not before I've gotten all the
info . . .)

Oh, these young people nowadays will try almost anything at least once, she says with an even smile which
freezes, freezes like her glazed eyes, her hands as, reassured
by her words and warmed by the booze he draws a comfort-
able sigh, leans back in the love seat, puts his feet on the
coffee table and proceeds to regale her with the most inti-

mate details of mixed and unmixed ecstasies à deux and a trois.

Drop dead, pig was all she could think as she sat frozen, a captive audience to Mr. Smut. No subtleties in his fat exposé. He was graphic. He omitted nothing. Oh, J! (Aunt V might say from far away to mom or the night) each time you disappear I'm doomed to watch a repeat performance of what went on at THE TROUBADOUR or THE TROM-BONE, A.C., D.C., wherever, I close my eyes and there you are, the three of you rolled into one hideous multi-limbed body like those statues they worship in India, hard core porn on the temple walls, lust minus love, I've written to my congressman for action, J, you've cheated on me with every bosomy fem, every rank male, my love, when I explore you with my tongue I make love to your female lovers, my jealousy becomes flesh. I make my jealousy work for me tooth and nail, tongue, nipples, knees and thumb all the way up the old ladder of ecstasy until my clitoris screams in a frenzy. Yes, J, each woman you've had in the flesh I've had in my mind, though when it comes to those rank hairy beasts, the mere thought of them turns me off and makes me throw up.

Remember our marriage vow! I heard her call from the talking room through the night. But mom was gone again and there was no one to hear her except myself through the walls or through the low rumble as a chunk of plaster fell from the ceiling in the condemned house next door.

Seems like that house may collapse without her having to

call in the wrecker. For now she wants it demolished. It is an eyesore, she says, and it has to come down before she puts our charming home on the market. Yes, she admits with a deep sigh of relief, she has decided to sell. A heartbreaking step, involving much soul searching. She has invested a lot of love in the house, a lot of money. The walls have listened to such intimate dramas she wonders what they might reveal if they could speak (or were bugged) though at this late stage in the game they have become like the walls of a tomb, what with J gone for so long by now it would be foolish to wait for her any further. It would be madness.

I've talked it over with my analyst, my astrologer too. For once they've come to the same conclusion: I've waited enough. Life must go on, for your sake and mine. Besides, this is an excellent time for selling. I need no couch or horoscope to help me interpret the market. Once the eyesore next door has been removed, the lot cleaned up and made attractive with a few plastic evergreens, a Disney dwarf or two, maybe a bird bath, I might sell the whole shebang as a package deal.

We'll move to the nest in the hills, she says, away from the perversions of the city, away from crime and sex, she says, lying down on the floor in her blue body stocking for keep-fit exercises, stretch, relax. Life on the farm is bound to be less strenuous, less hazardous for a growing girl like yourself. Now leave me to my yoga, baby. I've got to meditate before I sell.

Sell what, but I don't care. She sold me down the river. She wanted me to think that mom was dead when I knew she'd be back alive, I heard her bang at the boarded-up house and chant in the alley WHAT SHALL WE DO WITH THE DRUNKEN SAILOR, I heard her through the rain, I always will and it's Aunt V they may be carrying out in a box before long. Does she guess how many times I've shot her dead through the heart? The last time I gunned her down in my head was after the bad zoo trip. I conjured up Uncle D to visit with her and compare stocks over jasmine tea and toasted almonds. Delicious flavor. Crunch, slurp. BANG BANG. I shot her dead and sneaked the gun under his khaki bush shirt. The cops came jumping through the window to book him for homicide. But I saved him. I gave myself up.

Bang bang, Aunt V has promised me a wonderful wonder-bread time in the hills, no premarital sex in the hills, she says, not among the better classes, and we'll rate among the best now that your mom is gone.

Your mom is gone. I hate her when she says it, for gone sounds worse than dead, much further away, much more final. I don't believe a word she says and yet I begin to wonder what it was that made her decide to give up mom so suddenly from one day to the next. The house reminds me of a stopped clock. I ask myself why, but then it comes to me: the phones are no longer buzzing with false clues. She has changed to an unlisted number and she would also change the locks, she says, if she weren't going to sell soon, maybe sooner than expected. It won't take much time to demolish the house next door and clean up the mess. The man with the headache ball has promised to do his job tomorrow morning, she explains, checking the calendar. And all at once I have a suspicion that mom may really have left us for good, an empty feeling inside me as though my stomach had shriveled up never to be filled with food again.

Stop munching chocolates, please! She has thrown a mantilla over her head, a long black lace mantilla she bought with mom after their first bullfight in Barcelona. I'll run next door for a moment, she says (as if the abandoned house were inhabited and she were anxious to meet her neighbor!). No, dear, you mustn't come along. The whole place might collapse. I shouldn't take a chance myself, but I can't resist having a quick look around in case there's something there worth saving before the wreckers arrive.

Has she ever ventured inside the condemned house before? She can't remember. She's put on work gloves and I watch her knock off the boards in front of the entrance door which creaks open as the boards fall away with a clatter. In a moment she has disappeared in the gritty dust in the shadows and I count up to ten times ten and then climb after her, around a sawhorse and into a dim hall or room full of junk. The windows are boarded up and whatever little light there is comes through the cracks in those boards and through a fan light which casts a grimy purple dream glow over a wheeless baby buggy. I see Aunt V stand in a small room beyond, with her back turned to me and the ends of that lace mantilla from Barcelona in the dust underfoot as she points her electric torch like a gun at the wall before she lets it travel in a slow arc across the torn, faded wallpaper which has a flower pattern, I think of lilacs. She doesn't know I've followed her into the house and she is talking to herself in a low mumble that leaves no echo. I don't understand what she is saying. She has stooped to pick up an object—an old shoe? an old sneaker?—which she examines closely under the torch and then lets drop back on the floor. The way she stands there, straight again, and tall in that long, black mantilla, she might be in mourning for her favorite bullfighter, the one she and mom saw being disemboweled in the ring by one brave martyred bull. A bloody mess. The people made the matador into a saint. Aunt V sent his widow a halo of roses. But it's the bull who deserves the halo, I think as I watch her comb the rubble again, maybe for souvenirs from Barcelona.

There's the corpse of a mattress behind me and I flop down and try to think of Olli and me in the weeds. The mattress is littered with ancient magazines, chewed-up comic books, true crime or love, nothing worth saving from the wrecker, I guess until I see the message that's taped to superman with scotch tape so old it has turned the color of pure gold:

> WILL BE LATE
> DON'T YOU WAIT UP FOR ME

No signature. No love&kisses. The more I look at the scrap of paper the more the writing looks like mom's to me, though she's not one to leave messages. She just leaves. Still I will save that old copy of superman to ask her when she returns which may be any time, now or later, I think as I hear footsteps above my head. Aunt V must have gone upstairs with her electric torch. I listen closely. I watch the cracked ceiling come to life, the cracks spread under her heavy steps back and forth as the plaster dust, fine like mom's talcum powder, comes snowing down on me.

The walls seem to be shaking. A piece of plaster the size of my little finger drops on my shoulder and I jump up and hurry out of the death trap, almost a little sad as I think how Aunt V is sure to be buried by her own property.

The sky is hanging limp and gray like a wet sheet. I've rushed into the alley, and looking back I wait (still with that twinge of sadness but with a sudden crazy horror too like a wild joy) for the house to come crashing down. But it stands as it always has. And though I was inside it only seconds before, it already looks impenetrable again, a hundred times more secretive, I think as I shade my eyes against the gray glare of the sky. In a moment Aunt V has briskly stepped out of the shadows and toward our house. She is bareheaded now, and toting an old shopping bag she must have picked from the rubble. Her coif (drip-dry shake-it-yourself style for auburn brunettes created by our very own Mr. Clap of the Ritz à la Holstein) is sprinkled with plaster and maybe dry mouse shit, though the rest of her looks trim and cheery.

Hi, B! Want to see what Aunt V found in the junk?

She has sat down on our stoop with me, shopping bag between her knees which are spread out at an angle. Have rescued quite a few items, she says, from the greedy jaws of the grim shredder. The French call them OB-J TRUE-V, they can be fixed up or discarded (I mean the objects) or made over into something else. This broken peppermill for instance will make a cute toy for a needy minority child.

Reach into Santa's grab bag and what do we find? A noseless Lincoln bust, a busted guitar, an old sneaker; the single curved leg of a chair (but it's Hepplewhite, dear!). And goodness me, a genuine lace mantilla, very becoming.

Careful now—what's that? A beat-up spittoon.

Since mom has been crossed off her list (one mouth less to feed, she says, trying to make it sound like a joke though there is a sudden break in her voice and her eyes look empty) she may sell her business and retire. I've earned it, she adds weakly and I don't believe she believes it, I bet you she'll start a new business, an antique shop at granny-anny's place in the hills. Americana all over that part of the U.S.A. The local museum chock-full of slop jars, wagon wheels and rusty nails. I took a peek through the window with Olli. He said his granpa made a heap selling his old piss pot. Anything that isn't plastic must be antique. That's the glory of our country, it has such a short history each time you take a crap you are investing in Americana.

Aunt V is getting up from the stoop. Her joints are creaking. But she smiles. Once we have installed ourselves for good in the country and adjusted to a new routine, life will be so much healthier, more normal. She'll sketch and paint summer and winter. She'll putter about at her leisure, make things, fix things, sand the lovely oval frame (pure Americana) she found hanging empty upstairs in the condemned house. A picture frame, no doubt. But she will make it into a mirror and give it to one of the sisters for Valentine Day. She isn't absolutely sure which sister. But she has an idea.

The sky is flapping low and gray. We may have rain tonight, she says. Her nose twitches as she sniffs the wind and points the flashlight west in the direction of the river.

The searchlights from a waterfront patrol car sweep my window and break against my belly foamy white. My belly honeycombed with secret chambers floats on the night tide. Feel, sniff and lick. Dig for memory odors through secret crannies. The taste of semen on my tongue could mean it's a boy. Stop that, you tickle me, said Olli when I licked him up and down in the rain by the scrub oak. Dia de padre. Comes father's day I'll remember him with a rubber cigar C.O.D. and a Hallmark card anon: NOBODY TOPS MY POPS.

As yet no sex or name tag for my baby and O will have to do till I know more. O is a blank I can fill in with any shape or face I like. O might be an egg or the bald little spot atop Uncle D's head. O is that empty mirror frame Aunt V rescued from the wrecker. It was leaning against the mirror of the vanity table in the master or mistress bedroom where she had installed herself for the night earlier than usual amid violet sheets, throw pillows and the financial section of the N.Y.Times. She was reading up on REALTORS UNI- VERSAL (they've bitten the bullet, she smiled) and ringing for Flo to bring her the Ovaltine. Soothing potion for raw nerves. Make it a tall, tall glass.

Yes, ma'm.

O, I said into the mirror, addressing my baby, and Aunt V responded with Oregano, she likes to play word games, I don't, but I played along, I said Orgy and she said Order. Then I really socked it to her with Offals, Orgasm, Opium and Ovaries. Dear me, she said, you're getting too smart for me, Overkill and Oedipus is all I can come up with, and Ovaltine of course, thank you ever so much, Flo, would you mind awfully if I asked you to pick up my undies from under the vanity? Thanks a million. What a shame you don't care to move to the country with us. I would have sworn you'd jump at the occasion now that J is gone for good.

I told her what I thought of her and slammed the door behind me. Then I listened by the door: The child is terribly upset, Flo. That's natural. I am upset, Flo, terribly, terribly so. I and her mother were so very close, like sisters almost. And yet there is that certain relief, it came over me quite suddenly on the couch at my therapist's, an insight, Flo, a sense of liberation if you will . . .

Is there anything else, ma'm?

Hi, kid, mom whispered as she crept into my room out of the rain which had fallen through so many nights, had perhaps started that night when she had last disappeared, or so it seems to me now. Her rain-glazed face was swimming out of the door frame, toward my bed. And there was on her breath that mysterious odor I well remember from other nights when she'd surface after her trip through oblivion: an odor no longer of gin but of something more highly distilled, rarefied and almost otherworldly like a liquid reserved for angels.

Rain dripped from her poncho onto my face, my eyes as she was standing over me, trying to smile. Hi, kid. I said, hi, mom. It was that simple. We didn't carry on, we didn't kiss, and yes, it's always been that way, after each of her escapades when she'd creep home at last bone tired. We both would act as though she had never been further away than the pier or the nearest bar. And though I don't recall her having ever before come to my room first (usually she'd just collapse in the hall or on the bear rug) I still felt no surprise and asked no questions.

Hi, kid. My face was wet with rain. She was trying to smile. One of her front teeth was missing and I wondered had she been in a fight and had she saved the missing tooth to put under her pillow for the good fairy to find as I used to do with each of my milk teeth when I was a child.

Her face, like that of a tired child under the glistening poncho, was swaying above me in the wet light of the street lamp outside my window. Her knees were buckling and in a moment she had slid down on the rug by my bed and was fast asleep. I got up and managed to get her out of her wet things without waking her. I double wrapped her in my crazy quilt the way I would do with my dummy. I put my pillow under her head and kissed her good night.

Then I went back to bed, trying hard to stay awake to keep an eye on her. But I must have dozed off, for when I next looked she was no longer there and if it hadn't been for my pillow and quilt on the floor I might have thought I had dreamed up the whole scene.

The rain has almost stopped, I think. The foghorn has

stopped and the street lamp is swinging cool in the window to the hum of the river boats. BONNE NUIT CHERIE. The music sounds near enough to be coming from my little transistor. But it comes from our record player downstairs. Mom must have forgotten to shut my door, unless of course the wind blew it open.

The wind blows up against my neck. I'm drowsy. But I crawl out of bed. The crazy quilt in which mom had been sleeping is still warm and there is fine sand on it. Ocean sand? I walk across it barefoot, out of the room, to the stairs. There I sit down on the landing and look through the banister. The door to the talking room is standing open. The crystal chandelier is lit and mom and Aunt V come dancing out into the hall slowly, with their bodies melted together, their eyes shut.

BONNE NUIT CHERIE. The needle has made it over the scratch and the old record is turning smoothly again around and around.

About the Author

Born in Strasbourg, Alsace, Marianne Hauser has lived and worked in such diverse places as Bhavnagar, India and Greensboro, N.C.; Shanghai, China and Kirksville, Mo. Her present home is in New York where she writes, teaches, and studies under C.K. Chu at the Tai Chi Chuan Center. She is on the editorial board of *New Writers*, a magazine committed to the survival of the short story.

Her own short stories have been widely anthologized here and abroad, and collected in book form under the title *A Lesson in Music*. Her articles and literary criticism have appeared in leading magazines. Her novels include *Shadow Play in India, Dark Dominion, The Choir Invisible* which won her a Rockefeller grant, and *Prince Ishmael* which was nominated for the Pulitzer Prize and included by the New York Times Book Review on its Christmas List of the year's outstanding books.

FICTION COLLECTIVE

books in print:

The Second Story Man by Mimi Albert

Searching for Survivors by Russell Banks

Reruns by Jonathan Baumbach

Things In Place by Jerry Bumpus

Take It or Leave It by Raymond Federman

Museum by B. H. Friedman

The Talking Room by Marianne Hauser

Reflex and Bone Structure by Clarence Major

The Secret Table by Mark J. Mirsky

The Comatose Kids by Seymour Simckes

Twiddledum Twaddledum by Peter Spielberg

98.6 by Ronald Sukenick

Statements, an anthology of new fiction